Detroit
Stories Quarterly
Volume 8

Winter/Spring 2026

Shaping a Better Future

Our Stories

Our Voice

Our Way

DETROIT STORIES QUARTERLY, WINTER-SPRING 2026

Detroit Stories Quarterly is Published by:

40 Books Publishing

simgenenterprises@gmail.com

ISBN: 9798242585430

Our Stories

Like most things, Detroit was an idea first.

Before Dan Gilbert, before ruin porn, before Coleman Young, before Motown, before the Rebellion, before the Tigers won the World Series, before Hudson's, before Ford Motor Company, before Belle Isle, before Antoine de la Mother Cadillac.

Before it all.

Detroit was built by a collective imagination, at war with and in love with itself simultaneously. A perverse thing of beauty and horror, it has always been a city defined by dueling passions.

Detroit Stories is our attempt to expose both the beauty and the horror, the white hot friction of their coexistence that gave birth to an idea that some have mistaken for an illusion. But our city is no illusion, you just have to know what you're looking at. Otherwise you just might go blind and find yourself staring back at yourself through an empty funhouse mirror.

So here. Try these stories on for size. Now take another look. There. *Now* can you see it?

Thought so.

Keith Owens

Our Voice

What it is … What it was … What it Could be …
Detroit Stories Quarterly is a compelling statement. It says only *this* (or that) could have happened in the Motor City, but more importantly, the intent – and hopefully, the deep impact – of this experiment is acknowledging the imaginative engine driving its diverse citizenry. Today, it's hip to reference Detroit because of this apparent *resurgence* everyone's talking about. Fair enough. With all this national attention, other outlets are telling our stories: outsiders looking in. But Detroiters – and those native to the city – are the voices really qualified to tell the tale. It's a view from the inside, from the idea factory, unfiltered. The cross-pollination of blue/white/collar/industrialization/technological wonder. It's chili fry grease on the paper bag. Westside and eastside like two twin star systems derived from the same node.

Detroit is past, present and future occurring simultaneously, spinning simulacra like free verse in free fall. *Detroit Stories* should be speculative fiction and nonfiction at its very best. *Detroit Stories* will be the bus that always runs on time, where you can climb aboard, and yes, find a seat and watch the cityscape wiz by.

What it is … what it was … what it could be. *Detroit Stories* explores this and a whole lot more.

Cornelius Fortune

Our Way

Detroit's story

 it's hearkening to something glorious and wonderful and always

ALWAYS

In the process of becoming.

A **time**less entity transcending and bending

that is the essence of the mission we've undertaken.

We respect **time** and covet its good graces. In doing so we project ourselves fully

FULLY

Into and in to what is possible

BEYOND

The limits that have been previously imposed.

We ARE

The **timeless** journey of discovering and rediscovering

Detroit.

R.E. McTyre, Sr.

TABLE OF CONTENTS

Dedicated to the *future now* of Detroit

A note of appreciation to Maria Hauser for her copyediting.

All incidents and characters in the stories of this issue are wholly from the imagination of the authors and any resemblance to people living or dead is purely coincidental.

Detroit Stories Quarterly is published in Winter, Spring, Summer, and Fall.

Designer Dreams by Bob, Part II
by Keith A. Owens

7.

I was just a little girl, not more than nine or ten, when I first heard my Auntie talking about them. Auntie Pearl. She was the one Daddy never liked and always told Momma that he didn't want her inside his house, especially if I was at home. I still remember what he said to her the time he got mad. Daddy didn't get mad often, but when he did it was the kind of thing where you wanted to run somewhere and hide like you knew a storm was coming.

"I know she your sister, Lorraine. I *know* that. And you know I don't ever mean to get between you and your family, 'cause family's important. But Pearl is *crazy,* Lorraine. You know she is, and she bring that crazy with her. She just be wearing it."

And like all the other times, Momma nodded and swore Pearl wouldn't be back.

"Whenever I need to see Pearl about a thing, I'll go and see her instead," Momma promised.

And Daddy pretended to believe her, just like Momma pretended she was telling the truth. Looking back on it, I think Momma and Daddy needed the comfort of each other's lies, because the truth they were living with was just too terrible.

One week later, when Daddy was on the night shift at General Motors, Auntie Pearl was rocking back with

Momma on the porch. She was a big woman who liked to smoke cigars instead of cigarettes because she said men shouldn't be the only ones always to have life just the way they wanted it. To her, anyone could smoke a cigarette if they could afford to buy a pack, and anyone could afford to buy a pack of cigarettes if that's what they wanted. But not just anyone could afford a nice cigar. Cigars were made for special people, and Auntie Pearl refused to believe that men were the only special people in the world.

They were rocking back and forth real slow, in sync, not saying much. It was a humid summer evening and that's usually the way it was in weather like that. Everything moved slow in the heat and the damp, and conversations were short and to the point. I always felt like the only good thing about a hot day like that was waiting for it to cool off. Eventually, as the light drained from the sky, a breeze began to hiss its way through the trees. I listened, wondering if the wind would have any voice at all without leaves.

"Getting better now," said Momma.

Auntie Pearl uttered a noise from her throat indicating maybe she wasn't so sure. Momma picked up on it. I was sitting on the steps in front of them both, and I could feel Momma's question coming on because she could never let any doubt hang in the air.

"You don't think so, Pearl?" Momma asked, looking over at her sister who seemed to be staring at something far away.

Auntie Pearl rocked for nearly a minute longer before coming to a stop, and it seemed like she brought the whole evening to a stop with her. Suddenly, there wasn't any sound at all except our voices, like we were inside a padded room.

"I think they may be comin' tonight, Lorraine."

Momma drew a tight breath.

"Pearl, you know Sylvia sitting right there. She just a child and she don't need to hear . . ."

"She *do* need to hear, Lorraine! Just 'cause Jack always tellin' you how crazy I am don't make it true. Because you know it ain't. You and me grew up together in the same house, slept in the same bed all those years, and those dreams came for both of us at the same time."

"What dreams, Momma?" I asked, knowing I was never supposed to interrupt when grown folks were talking but I couldn't help myself, sensing that whatever secrets they were trying to hide were somehow tied to my own.

"See what you done, Pearl? Now you got Sylvia asking questions about things she don't need answers to. Not yet."

"How you know she—"

"Momma sometimes I have dreams too."

I had never seen a look like that before on my mother; an all-encompassing fear that worked the flesh around her eyes and the hard lines in her dark chocolate face. But Auntie Pearl looked calm. She began to nod, and as she did, the padded room that felt like it had been surrounding us fell away in ragged pieces. I could hear the crickets, and ribbons of smoke from her cigar crept upward into the night air.

"Jesus God help me," I heard Momma whisper.

Auntie Pearl reached over and, real gentle, placed her hand over her sister's.

"The longer you keep that knowledge from your daughter, my niece, the longer that child be in trouble. Because it's not knowing, and not believing, that's what gives them their powers."

Momma looked like she was about to say something, but she squeezed her eyes shut and mashed her lips together. She shook her head slow and I could hear her groan, like there was a growing pain deep inside.

"Who are the night people, Auntie Pearl?"

For a while, I thought maybe she wasn't gonna answer me. And her being an adult and my aunt, I knew I couldn't press. Just had to wait for it.

Turns out, neither my mother nor Auntie Pearl had ever really *seen* the night people. At least not directly. Because they weren't the sort to ever exist directly in front of you where you could see them for what they were. They existed as shadows and blurs shimmering at odd angles and in the far corners of your vision, right where you thought you saw something but then . . . just beyond that. Always teasing, making you question what you knew to be true—even if you didn't want it to be.

"They the ones take you to your dreams. Like escorts," she said, answering my question. But when I responded that I was already dreaming without any escorts, she shook her head as her eyes focused on the darkness, as if waiting for something to step through.

"Just because you dream doesn't mean those dreams are yours, and just because you close your eyes don't mean you asleep. Those dreams you been having, how long has it been?"

"Maybe a year."

"Hmm. And what is it that you dream? Can you remember any of them, or do they fade away? Because most people's dreams, they fade away after a while."

"I remember all of them," I said. "But especially I remember the dream I had last night."

"Jesus God . . ." my mother said.

"It's all right, Lorraine. Better we have this talk now, so she knows what to do when the time comes."

Auntie Pearl focused back on me.

"Tell me about the last dream you had," she said.

Momma started to interrupt.

"Was there a—"

"Let her tell it, Lorraine. We gotta let her tell it. Only chance we have of this working out like it should."

"You were gonna ask me about the gray man, weren't you, Momma?" I asked, feeling a chill come over me.

Auntie Pearl looked at Momma and nodded.

"Yes," she said after a beat, her voice sounding choked.

He was there, but it wasn't the first time. Only it was the first time he ever spoke to me, or even acted like he saw me at all. Most times I would see the gray man he would just be floating, like he wasn't really paying attention to much of anything. Not to me or to anything. But wherever I was, he was always there. Sometimes right above my head like a cloud, murmuring nonsense I couldn't understand, then other times far away, maybe sitting in a tree or on top of a building. Staring off into the distance.

I was scared of him at first, and one time I even tried running away. Like how you run away from things when you're in a nightmare and you can't get up any real speed. I think maybe he knew I was scared because in that dream, it lasted a lot longer than most of the others, he disappeared. Or made me think that he had disappeared because I didn't see him anywhere. But then I started noticing that everything around me was turning gray, and I could hear this funny-sounding laughter, like it was coming out of a tin can. But instead of getting scared, I got mad and I started cursing him. Then I woke up.

The next dream I had was the one where he spoke to me. It was normal in a way, like how things are in the waking world. I thought maybe I wasn't dreaming for what felt like a long while. I was sitting on a green bench in a huge park, looking down a hill full of swaying green grass at a lake that was perfectly round and perfectly still. For some reason the lake's appearance made me smile, and then laugh, but quietly. I was the only person in this park with the perfect circle of a lake under a perfect Easter eggshell blue sky patched with cotton ball clouds.

Then everything shimmered the way heat does when you can see it rising off of asphalt in the summertime, making the world waver. I tilted my head to the side, trying to figure out what had happened.

"That never works," he said.

The gray man was sitting next to me on the bench, only not quite on the bench. He was cross-legged and hovering not more than an inch above, looking down toward the circle lake. I probably should have been surprised, maybe even frightened, and would have been frightened for sure if it hadn't been a dream, which now I knew that it was. The gray man had unnaturally smooth skin the color of putty, and there were no creases or lines to be found anywhere on his naked form. But only naked because he wore no clothes, not like how a person would look if naked, and that's why I didn't feel any awkwardness or shame as he sat there with no visible eyes or ears or nose or sex—just a gray form, kind of like a mannequin.

"Why?" I asked.

"Because it takes more than tilting your head one way or the other to change the world, don't you think?"

I nodded.

"I guess."

We sat there awhile longer before I noticed the small ripples beginning to form across the surface of the lake, like what you would see once a breeze had started to blow - except there was no breeze. Everything else was still.

Soon the ripples became waves, and then . . .

"I saw them."

Auntie Pearl sat up straight in her chair, giving me a hard look. She took a deep draw on her cigar, then slowly blew out the smoke.

"You saw *them?*"

"But baby, you can't see—"

Auntie Pearl raised her hand up like she was stopping traffic and that traffic was a train. Momma's mouth stayed open but the words stuck in her throat.

I nodded.

"Yes ma'am. I did. I mean, I didn't know until just now that's who—what . . . ? What they were. But I saw them in the dream. The water in that lake started rippling, and at first I thought maybe there was a breeze down there that I couldn't feel where I was sitting, but then the ripples got to be more like waves, and then they started to act funny, not like how you see them do in the ocean or in any lake you've ever seen."

"Funny how?"

"They weren't going in the same direction, Auntie. At first they were, and like I said, I thought maybe it was a different sort of breeze down there. But then, once those ripples got bigger into waves, they started turning against each other—like they didn't like each other. It was like the waves were *attacking* each other. I remember I wanted to ask the gray man what was happening, but when I tried to turn my head to look at him it was like my neck was locked and I couldn't look one way or the other except at what was happening in the lake.

And then . . .

8.

"I think they may be comin' tonight, Lorraine."

Auntie Pearl was right. Why they chose that particular night, I'm not sure, but one thing I do know for sure is those things knew how to make an entrance.

It was happening again, the same way it did in my dream, with the round lake somehow appearing in front of us where the street should have been. Where the car should have been parked. Where that raggedy house across the street should have been, right next to that lot full of toddler-high weeds where that other house had been torn down a few years back.

And there *he* was, the gray man, hovering in front of us above the porch steps with his arms clasped behind him. I should have been scared.

"I believe you cursed me the last time we met," he said, acting as if my aunt and my mother weren't there.

I shook my head.

"No. It was the time before that. Last time was when we were seated on that bench. We were talking about things."

"Yes! That's right, that's right. We were near the lake."

"As a matter of fact it was . . . nevermind. Why are you here? And why are you bringing my family into this? I thought my dreams were mine."

"What makes you think this is a dream? Aren't you sitting here on the porch right now, as you have been all evening long, with your Aunt and your mother?"

"Yes. Which is why *you* don't belong. *So why are you here?*"

The gray man had no features on his face; no mouth, no nose, no eyes. And yet I had this for sure feeling that he was smiling.

"Lorraine? You haven't told her yet, have you?" he said.

"She just tryin' to protect her daughter, demon!" yelled Auntie Pearl. "Ain't no need for you to be starting this mess all over again."

And that's when my mother's mouth turned into a zipper, I think maybe to punish Auntie Pearl who cried out in pain as if she had been stabbed. She reached over to stroke her sister's cheek. Momma's eyes grew real big while she tugged frantically at the slider on the left side of where her mouth had been. I could feel my body starting to tremble and shake. I tried to say something to comfort my mother but could only stutter and spit.

"I would advise you to stop pulling on your zipper and accept your temporary fate. You do not want to see what might come out of your mouth if you disregard my warning."

Then he leaned forward, and I could feel he was still smiling on that blank slate of a face.

"But then maybe you need a little more than my warning. Perhaps you don't believe that I am only trying to consider your best interests. So then allow me to allow *you* to witness the consequences of disobedience, Lorraine. Because I happen to know, same as your sister Pearl knows, that you were not always one to heed instruction as a child growing up. Isn't that right, Pearl?"

Auntie Pearl opened her mouth to respond, and I could tell it would have been a ripper, but the gray man raised a warning finger into the air.

"*Think*. Before you speak. Now is there still something you wish to say? Because I wasn't asking your opinion, dear Pearl. I don't *care* about your opinion."

Auntie Pearl sat back further in her chair. She was trying not to look afraid, probably for my sake, but I could tell that she was.

"Just don't hurt my sister. Please," she said.

"I am merely trying to assist your sister so that she does not harm *herself.*"

And with that, the left corner of the zipper that had become my mother's mouth pulled open halfway, revealing a dark hole that bore no resemblance to a mouth but more like a small cave. From inside the cave, distant at first, I could hear otherworldly screeches and wailings. Within moments, those hellbound noises grew louder as my aunt's fear-crazed eyes stretched open wider. She began to tremble and shake so hard I thought she might hurt herself. She was trying to scream, but instead could only choke on whatever was making its way toward the dark exit in her face.

"Stop. *Please,*" I said.

But the gray man just sat there in mid-air, hovering and observing the spectacle as small grayish green tentacles with blood red suckers attached began to force their way through the opening in my mother's face, twisting it open wider and wider until everything was grotesquely out of proportion.

The gray man snapped his fingers.

"That should do it, I think," he said.

The screeches escalated to a near-deafening level as whatever was on the other end of those tentacles was suddenly being sucked back into the abyss against its will. The appendages whipped back and forth in a frenzy, the suckers on one particularly stubborn tentacle attempting to attach themselves to the bottom of where her lip had been to prevent its return to wherever it had come from - but without success. Still, it managed to leave a saucer-shaped scar that never fully healed.

The zipper closed, and the night was silent once again.

"So then are we at an understanding?" asked the gray man.

All three of us nodded our heads. Tears ran down my mother's face, and Auntie Pearl made a move to give comfort, but once again the gray man raised a narrow, smooth digit in warning. He shook his head in slow motion.

"Let's just remain where we are, shall we? And now, there is a group of someones I would like for you to meet. That you need to meet. They have been a part of your family for quite some time, going back generations upon generations, but have always kept themselves just out of sight, as is their way. And per protocol. But it is apparent that the time has come for you to meet the Noct. They are also known as the Night People, and they have been assigned to your family's line since its beginning."

With that terrifying introduction, the dark waters of the lake began first to steam and bubble as if in a huge cauldron, then to swirl faster and faster as if being stirred by a giant invisible spoon. There was a high-pitched whirring noise that grew stronger with an irritating intensity to the point where I had to clap both hands over my ears, and so did my mother and Auntie Pearl. The gray man remained still and floating on his mid-air perch, keeping watch on the impossibility of a scenario that we were all witnessing until what looked like a long, shiny thin talon pushed its way through the surface of the churning waters, extending its length toward the firmness of the street at its border where it found purchase. It was maybe three feet in length, only a few inches in width, and so dark in color that it looked more like an accidental ragged tear in the night. Soon there was another, followed by a third, with the high-pitched whirring growing increasingly unbearable until . . .

And then it stopped. The lake shriveled and folded itself up and out of existence, and standing in its place were three extremely tall, wraith-like figures, their bodies twisted and broken at painful angles. They seemed to shimmer in and out of form, like the heat waves rising from a noontime highway in the dead of summer. Their eyes, red and ragged, were focused intently on the three members of my family, all of whom had aged an eternity with fear in only a matter of hours.

Employing that same smooth digit that he had used to warn my aunt from comforting her own sister, the gray man motioned to the beings.

"Come," he said, his voice sounding strained but also urgent.

"Come."

And with that, the three nightmare figures assumed a more solid shape before taking a unitary, noiseless step forward. The absence of sound as the Noct began to move in our direction caused my heart to beat so hard against my ribcage that it felt like it was trying to escape.

"Stop," I whispered, before I realized I was saying anything.

For the first time that night, the gray man appeared unsettled from his floating perch. He turned suddenly to face me, and I could feel a simmering heat reaching out from his direction. He shook his head slowly, as if in warning. But I didn't care.

"Stop," I said again, only louder. This time, I recognized a deeper, echoing quality in my voice that seemed to be coming from somewhere else - even if that somewhere was somewhere else inside of me.

And as if they had suddenly found themselves trapped in tar, all three of the night people found themselves locked in place, unable to take another step forward. They began to moan and wail, then to sway back and forth. As for myself, I could slowly feel my fear begin to leak away. I stared directly back into the blank face of the gray man, who was now shaking his head back and forth furiously.

"No. NO! You CAN'T!" he said, his voice taking on a bizarre, metallic quality totally in contrast to the calm, controlling tone he had been flaunting moments earlier.

I smiled, turned to let my mother and aunt see that I was smiling, then returned my focus to the gray man who was now shaking radically back and forth like the rattles on the tail of a snake.

"But I think I can," I said, keeping my voice calm and serene. "And I think I know why. You want to know why? Because this is a dream too, isn't it? I let you make me think that you had somehow managed to step into my real world, when all you did was put me to sleep. I'm sleeping right now, aren't I, Mr. Gray Man? Right here on my front porch, I am sleeping, which means this is my dream, which means . . . yes. Momma? You're OK."

"NOOOOOOO!"

"Yes."

And with that, the fullness of my mother's beautiful lips returned as her fingers began to explore the thankful familiarities of her dark brown face without a zipper.

"Oh . . . my sweet baby . . ." she blurted out in joyful surprise.

Feeling my strength surging back into me like electricity, I pointed toward the street, then began to stir my finger in a circle, creating an invisible 'O' in the air. Soon the grotesque improbability of the circular lake appeared once again in the middle of the street, its waters angrily spinning into a funnel.

"I believe it's time for you all to go back home," I said, then watched happily as my nightmare creatures were yanked into the hungry mouth of the waters and swallowed whole.

Next thing I knew, my mother and Auntie Pearl were kneeling beside me on the porch, shaking me as hard as they could.

"I *see* you, baby. I *see you*. We *both* see you, Sylvia. Come back to us, now, hear? *Come back to us.*"

9.

And soon enough, I did come back, Randall. I had every reason to think that just by my waking up - and because of all my dreamtime heroics - that we were all safe and sound because I had miraculously saved the day and vanquished the evildoers. But the look in my mother's eyes told me different.

"What . . . ?" I asked, my voice sounding surprisingly hoarse. "How long was I gone?"

My mother and Auntie Pearl exchanged looks, which gave me a chill inside.

"What?" I asked again, this time more insistent.

"Baby, you're not all the way out. You're just at the next level of dreaming. But we're gonna make a way. Just you hang on, and don't give up. We're here now."

"But if I'm just at another level of dreaming, then what about . . ."

"We're here now."

*****

It took another week before my mother and your great aunt found that way out they had promised me. And the truth of it is, looking back? I don't think they actually knew - or maybe even didn't believe - that they would ever find that way out of the second level of dreaming. Because they knew the stories about those who never woke up, who got lost in the maze of the dreaming. Some got caught between levels, while others got stuck on a level where the exits were never really exits but only interwoven tunnels that took them deeper and deeper into the dream.

But what they did was to actually negotiate a deal with the night people that somehow allowed them to wake up and return to the real world. How they managed to make contact with them without engaging the gray man is something I never quite understood, but I do know it was a deal that made him angry because it took away from his powers.

And that's not the only thing I know. And here is where I need to ask forgiveness for your grandmother and your great aunt, and for you to understand that the deal they made, even though it freed us, was also flawed. But I will always believe they had hope - a belief even - that down the line, the mistake they allowed themselves to make would be corrected by either you or me. And they also had hope that, as family, we would understand why they had to make the concession that they did. Because if they hadn't made that agreement with the night people then you never would have been born and I'm not sure what would have happened to me as the young child of a mother who would never wake up again.

*****

"What was the deal that they made?" I asked.

It was close to 3 o'clock in the afternoon of that same Tuesday when Mom had fixed me those pancakes, and I had devoured them like they were the last pancakes on Earth. Actually, that's what Mom had said - what she *always* said - whenever she watched me eating her pancakes.

Only this morning was different. Which was why, nearly six hours later, Mom and I were still sitting across from one another at the kitchen table. Mom was looking at her hands as they fidgeted in a way that emphasized how uncomfortable she was. She stared at them hard, as if she didn't quite recognize those appendages as belonging to her. Or maybe she thought by staring at them hard enough, they might finally act *as if* they belonged to her, instead of endlessly tapping and drumming out of time.

And as hard as she was staring at her disobedient fingers, I was staring at my mother. Because never before in my 16 years as her child could I remember her ever being anything but in control. Not like a dictator, but exactly the way you figure mothers are supposed to be. Protective if she thought anything threatened me, soothing

26

when she could sense my heart starting to race. Mom always seemed to have the answers to whatever it was. She just *knew*.

But that particular afternoon was the first time I witnessed my mother so rattled. Everything she told me that day, that came spilling out of her like dark waters breaking through a dam, scared the hell out of me. But not so much that I didn't want to know more. Because I needed to.

"What was the deal they made?" I asked again.

A small tear leaked from the corner of her eye and rolled down her cheek as she shook her head.

"All they wanted was to get home, Randall. You have to understand that. All they wanted was to get home. Because they made themselves believe that once they got home, they could fix it. Whatever it was. But if they got stuck in those dreams . . . ?"

I knew the only thing I could do was to let the silence hang there for a long while, and not to interfere. Because the silence was a temporary protection from the horrors of the truth. I was safe so long as my mother didn't complete her sentence, but eventually the time did come.

"I need to know," I said, realizing my voice must have sounded unsure, reflecting how I felt. But regardless of that, Mom nodded.

"The deal was that the Night People would be granted access to the dreams of our family through the end of our line. For as long as our name breathes, the Night People have permission to enter and exit the dreams of our family, and to design them, as they please."

10.

"I need to take a trip, Randall."

"Not without me, you aren't."

"If I take you, the trip will be for nothing. Because if he has both of us then what kind of leverage is that? We'll both be stuck in his maze with no way out. I remember the stories my mother and Aunt Pearl told me about what that was like, and it's nothing either of us should want any part of."

The sun was going down, closing out what had actually been a nice fall day. Not too many clouds, just a bit of a breeze. The kind of day you know how to value if you live in Michigan, where you spent two-thirds of the year waiting for days like these. Both of us were sitting at the kitchen table looking out the window at the back yard fence. It needed a new paint job, but I had never been the kind who was inclined to do that sort of home repair. Neither was my mother.

"So where is this trip gonna take you?" I asked as my stomach clinched like a fist, wondering if maybe I wouldn't see her again. She said the risk was greater if the both of us went, but I had to wonder what was to keep the Gray Man from settling for one if he couldn't have us both. Because I knew it was the Gray Man she was going to see.

"I'm not sure yet. The only way I can reach out to him is in the dreaming, not while we're awake. Which is another reason why I need for you to stay behind and not come with me. I need an anchor on *this* side, if you know what I mean."

"I'm not sure I do."

She nodded slowly.

"I'm not real sure I do either. Only that if it looks to you - or more important, *feels* to you - like something isn't right while I'm gone, then you'll do whatever you have to do to bring me back. It may mean bringing me back in bad shape, or even dead but . . ."

"*Dead?*"

'Shhh. Listen to me, Randall. I don't expect that to happen, but it's better I'm dead and on *this* side than alive and trapped in the dreams. And don't ask me what it is you'll need to do because I don't know. You'll just have to figure it out."

"Right. Figure it out."

My voice sounded snappish and sarcastic, but I couldn't help it. I was scared and angry at the same time, and my mother was making the possibility of her death sound as routine as a trip to the grocery store where you couldn't find the mayonnaise. She reached across the table and squeezed my forearm gently, then rubbed her thumb back and forth across the skin. Nothing like a mother's touch. She tried to smile, and I placed my hand over hers.

"I'll figure it out."

*****

I was more scared than I let on to Randall, or at least that I thought I was letting on. My son's always been the type who was too good at picking up signs about things, and he could usually read me like a book. But later that night as he sat in the chair beside my bed, looking down at me and holding my hand? Well, if he *did* know I was putting on the brave face then he was doing just as good an acting job as I'd like to think that I was.

"I'll be right here when you get back," he said. "No matter how long it takes, Mom. OK? I'll be here. I'm not going anywhere."

We smiled at each other for what felt like a long while in the dim light of my bedroom, which was only lit by the damned near ancient lamp perched by my bedside on the equally ancient wooden table like a small vulture. I remember wondering to myself when was I ever going to replace that thing, then suddenly being whisked away into darkness. Something was tugging me into the void. Randall's gentle face was disappearing rapidly, and I tried to reach out and touch my baby one more time but then he was gone and the darkness was complete.

The first thing I noticed after what felt like hours of descent was that there were no colors here. No sound either, at least not like what you would notice on the other side. It's funny how you don't miss some things in your life because they're always there - until they're not. And in this place where everything was some shade of gray, the absence of any familiar sounds made my heart start to race. I would have given anything to hear the rumble of a car engine or the chirping of a bird. A dog barking. The wind.

Instead, I could feel the silence pressing in, trying to find a way inside my head. To fight it off, I walked forward into the vast expanse of nothingness that stretched itself outward in every direction into the distance of what vaguely resembled a horizon. I forced myself to remember all the colors that I had ever seen and all the sounds of life that I could recall. I soon realized there were no smells either, so as I continued to press forward for no other reason than it seemed like a better idea than standing still, I drew on memories of Auntie Pearl's Thanksgiving dinners, and my mother's peach cobbler that she made from scratch. I conjured memories of the sometimes odd, nose-wrinkling smells in our backyard and in the alley that ran behind the house. I would have given anything to experience those again.

But for what felt like days of endless walking, the closest I was allowed to come to real life were the images stored inside my head. For one stretch of my journey I kept my eyes closed, thinking maybe that would bring my memories closer to the surface, perhaps even manifest in the wasteland surrounding me. But the longer my eyes were closed the more the gray seeped behind my eyelids, flushing those memories away piece by piece. And so I resolved to keep them open no matter what.

Which turned into what could have been days and then weeks, maybe longer. But strangely I never felt the need to sleep, or even to rest. I didn't get tired, nor did I feel hungry. I only knew that I needed to keep walking if I wanted to stay alive, to keep moving at all costs. Because standing still in the Gray Man's dream - what this had to be - was likely a form of death, even though moving forward was neither forward nor backward nor anywhere at all because there was no way to judge any form of progress in any direction. It was like being on a treadmill.

"I refuse to go crazy," I said, muttering the first words I had spoken since my arrival.

The cackling sound of his laughter, which suddenly erupted all around me, chilled me to the bone. And then he mocked me.

I refuse to go crazy! I refuse to go crazy!

The voice, like a high-pitched parrot, echoed in the air surrounding me. For the first time since I had started my long walk, I stopped. I looked around at the emptiness for any indication of where the sound had come from but there was no clue. The fear I felt morphed into anger, but I knew I had to control it. Give this thing any hint that I was becoming unraveled and it would pull me apart right there on the spot. Of that much I was certain. This was the Gray Man's dream, not mine, and he was still angry.

"It wasn't me, you know. I'm glad they did it, and I guess it's too bad for you to get embarrassed like that, the way they worked around you with the Night People, but it doesn't change the fact it wasn't me. Whatever anger you have, you need to take that up with my mother and my Aunt."

The silence was immediate and brutal. After awhile, I started to think maybe I should start walking again, but that would be giving up and I had already come too far and taken too much of a risk. Then, in the distance, I could see a road beginning to form. An empty two-lane highway unfurling itself toward me like a carpet at a rapid pace through the expanse until it stopped soundlessly a few feet in front of me. Moments later, I saw the Gray Man strolling toward me down that road. I was used to him simply appearing or hovering, so this was strange. I was determined he wasn't gonna see me sweat, so as he got closer I cocked my head to the side and forced myself to smile.

"Hi there," I said.

He stopped, and I could sense his curiosity, which I took as a good thing. Then, right there in mid-air, he folded his legs upward and positioned himself on an invisible plateau, placed his hands in his lap, then also cocked his head to the side. Such a mimic. He was probably mimicking my smile too, but since he had no face there was no way to tell.

"A brave little girl you are," said a voice inside my head.

"Not a little girl anymore though. You should remember that."

The amused laughter resembled the rattle of a snake.

"A peacock then. Strutting your colorless feathers in a dream that isn't even yours."

"The drab gray was your choice, not mine. If this is the way you like to live, then good for you. But can we quit this? You need to know why I'm here, because if I could be anyplace else in the world, believe me I would be."

The rattling sound again, a little louder, followed by an extended hiss.

"This? This is not the world. At least not as you know it. This is something else entirely. Perhaps you were mistaken about your destination?"

I could feel my heart starting to race, but I was hoping my heightened anxiety didn't show. I shook my head.

"No. I'm in the right place because you're here. Acting the way you always do. You need to know why . . ."

"I'm well aware of why you're here, Sylvia. Like I said, this is not the world as you know it. There are no secrets hidden from me here. Only from you. You're here as a mother, is that correct?"

"It is."

"Hmmm. Yes. You were smart not to bring the boy. But then again, maybe not? Because what makes you think . . ."

"That you won't settle for one if you can't have both. Right. I already considered that. Guess there are some secrets you don't know about down here after all."

The sudden silence felt full of poison but now was too late to panic. That realization alone made me calm.

"He's just a 16-year-old boy who has nothing to do with any of this. For all these years you've been controlling his dreams, turning them into nightmares for your own amusement. Because you're still so mad that my mother and Aunt Pearl escaped from your maze right out from under you with the Night People's help. So you're taking your anger out on a child. That's it, isn't it? The grownups are out of your reach so instead you figure it's easier to pick on someone your own size. Someone small. That really is a shame, isn't it? How you just can't seem to measure up?"

"I would be careful if I were you, Sylvia. I believe it is you who needs me, not the other way around."

That was true, but I could feel him getting unsettled which could work to my advantage. At least I thought maybe it could. I was on unfamiliar territory, so nothing was certain.

"Fine. I'll be careful. So then what is it you're getting from all this? What wealth is there in infecting a child's dreams? Oh, and I'm assuming you know Randall by now is almost numb to your meddling. You beat someone long enough and there comes a time when the pain starts to become normal."

"So then why are you here, dearest? If Randall no longer feels any discomfort, then it seems to me like this is a wasted visit on your part."

"Because, you sick and twisted being, no child should feel living with nightmares is normal."

"Ah. I see. Well I suppose that does make a bit of sense."

"So then what are you going to do about it?"

The Gray Man took a deep breath, then put his head in his hands as if he were contemplating something. He held that pose for several minutes, not flinching, like a statue. Then he uttered a slight cough before clearing his throat.

"I don't plan to do anything at the moment. But there will come a time, some years from now, once Randall becomes grown, when he will encounter someone who should be able to deliver him. Help him to control his dreams, to be the master of his dreamstate fate, if you will. But until that time comes?"

The Gray Man shrugged his shoulders, then giggled. "Goodbye, Sylvia."

Wait.

CONCLUSION
The Dream Rider

Then came a sudden rush of air whistling by my ears as everything began to twist out of shape, like a Salvador Dali. Slowly it all began to spin in a wide circle in a way that reminded me of the tumbling shapes and colors inside a washing machine. The woman, who had appeared to me full-bodied with caramel brown skin and shiny bronze eyes, was swallowed into the mad swirl of it all as her outstretched arm became distorted and twisted into a flapping, rubbery appendage that hardly resembled anything belonging to a human being. Her mouth stretched open wide until it seemed wide enough to consume her entire body, and then it did.

Remember, this dream was designed for you. It can't harm you, only soothe you. And you have complete control.

"STOP," I yelled, as loud as I could.

And then it did. Like a freeze frame in a movie, everything stopped right where it was. There was no sound, no smell, no nothing. Just me, looking at a dream interrupted.

You have complete control.

"Make it like it was. And bring her back. I want to know who she is and where she was taking me."

There was the immediate sensation of butterfly wings brushing my fingers, followed by her beautiful smiling face only inches from mine, bronze eyes glowing.

"That's better," she said. "Now come."

Midnight Mercy

By R.E. McTyre, Sr.

Smoke Over Hastings Street

Detroit was never quiet, not even in winter. The forges still burned, the streets still rattled with trolleys and ten thousand dreams hammering at steel. By '42, we were a city at war—factory floors turning from sedans to bombers, and everyone pretending not to see the cracks widening under the strain.

My name's Langston Reed, though most folks know me by the voice I give to *The Midnight Detective*, that radio mystery running every Thursday on WJLB. They say I sound like I know things. Like I've seen the dark side of a man's soul and still believe there's a light somewhere past it. Maybe that's because I have.

I live right off Hastings Street, above a tailor shop that smells of starch and cigar smoke. From my window, I can see the shadow of Paradise Valley spreading out like a velvet glove—clubs, pool halls, sanctuaries, sin, and salvation all stitched into one crooked smile. The air tastes like brass and bourbon, the soundtrack of people trying to survive the American dream.

When I'm not writing radio mysteries, I'm often with Captain Henry Mercer, head of detectives down at the Twelfth Precinct. We met years back when I was stringing for the *Detroit Tribune*, before the scripts and sponsors took over my typewriter. Mercer's a white man with more conscience than most—an old Irish cop who learned to listen before he judged. He says my instincts help him read the angles nobody else sees. I say it's just what the Spirit lets me see when I'm quiet enough to notice.

That Thursday night in January, I'd just finished dictating an episode called *Murder in the Factory District* when Mercer's call came through. His voice had that familiar gravel edge—half fatigue, half trouble.

"Langston," he said, "I've got a body down by the Rouge Plant. Looks like another worker accident. Only I don't buy it. You free?"

I looked at the half-empty glass of Coca-Cola beside my typewriter, the pages of dialogue still warm from the ribbon. "You know me, Cap," I said. "For a friend, I'm always free."

The Ford River Rouge Plant was a cathedral of metal: miles of conveyor belts and furnaces, glowing like the gates of judgment. The war had made it holy ground. Men and women, Black and white, worked side by side building B-24 Liberators, though not all of them earned the same respect or pay.

By the time I got there, the night air was thick with smoke and steam, the kind of cold that cuts your teeth when you breathe. Mercer stood by the loading docks with two uniformed men. A body lay half-hidden under a tarp.

"Name's Elias Booker," Mercer said. "Colored. Line worker. Found him near the freight elevator. The plant foreman says it was an accident. A fall. But Booker's brother insists he was pushed."

I crouched near the tarp, feeling the weight of silence. The man's face bore no peace, just the stiff mask of a final question. "He's young," I said. "Late twenties?"

"Twenty-six. Good worker, clean record."

"And his brother?"

"Works the same line. Says Elias was talking about a war contract scam. Something about parts going missing, money changing hands."

Corruption in the war effort was nothing new. To their credit, Washington was trying to crack down on it. There was this brash young senator from Missouri, Harry S Truman, who'd been put in charge of it. His committee had already won some indictments, and word was, there were more to follow.

But for a Black man to know too much about it? That was a death sentence dressed as an accident. Mercer sighed and lit a cigarette. "City's boiling, Langston. We're building planes to fight tyranny overseas while half this town can't walk down Woodward without being reminded what color they are."

He wasn't wrong. You could hear it in the way people spoke. Hope tightening into bitterness, faith turning to fury. Detroit was a fuse waiting for a match. There was this new organization that had come along a few years ago, the National Association for the Advancement of Colored People, that was trying to bring attention to the problem. But they had their hands full these days just dealing with all the lynchings that were taking place down South.

As we walked through the plant, I let my intuition breathe. My grandmother used to call it *the listening spirit.* "When a man's quiet enough," she'd say, "the Lord will whisper what eyes can't see."

And that night, I felt it—an unease beneath the clang of steel. Something crooked was hiding in the rhythm of honest work.

We found Booker's locker. Inside were two things: a torn photograph of a woman holding a child, and a folded page from a company ledger—half burned, as if someone tried to erase the proof.

Numbers, signatures, missing inventory lines. Someone was stealing from Uncle Sam, and Elias Booker had stumbled into it.

Mercer glanced at me. "Think it's worth pushing?" I met his eyes. "If a man dies for the truth, the least we can do is listen to it."

He nodded. "You'll help me?"

I nodded affirmatively, "I already am."

As I left the plant, the city felt heavier than before—smokestacks rising like questions, each one waiting for an answer only faith or fire could give.

I didn't know it yet, but the case of Elias Booker would drag me into a world of greed and shadow where mercy came at midnight—and sometimes, not at all.

The Body Beneath the Bell

The next morning brought snow, soft and mean as sugar over ice. Detroit's chimneys exhaled a gray breath that never seemed to end, and the newspapers shouted headlines about the Pacific front and patriotism. The African American papers, *The Michigan Chronicle* and *The Vigilante*, were rich with personal stories about families on the homefront, and with excerpts from letters from servicemen and women writing home. Down on Hastings, though, the talk wasn't about the war—it was about Elias Booker, and whether a Black man's death in a war plant meant anything at all.

I walked to the Starlight Diner on Mack Avenue, where Mercer liked his eggs hard and his coffee strong enough to take paint off a Buick. He was already there, coat open, tie undone, eyes reading something behind the newsprint.

"You didn't sleep," I said.

He folded the paper. "Neither did you."

"Booker's death is bothering you."

"You could say that," he grunted. "The coroner's calling it accidental, but the report stinks—blunt trauma to the back of the head, wrong angle for a fall. The plant manager wants it closed before Washington hears."

"Because of the war contracts."

"Because of the money," Mercer said flatly. "Everything else is just flag dressing."

I took out the torn ledger page we'd found in Booker's locker. The burnt edge left a bite mark through the signature, but you could still read most of it. Parts missing from shipments, units overbilled. A name caught my eye—L. C. Whitmore, Supply Supervisor.

Whitmore was a name I'd heard before—once, whispered at the *Blue Lantern Club*, a jazz joint where rumors flowed faster than gin.

"I know someone who might help," I said. "But she'll want to be asked right."

Mercer gave me that look he saved for when my friends operated in corners the badge couldn't reach. "Just don't get yourself in too deep, Langston."

"Cap, I live in deep water," I said, a little cockier than I should have. "I just learned how to float."

****

The Blue Lantern sat in the basement of a grocery on St. Antoine, a place where you could hear the war and forget it all at once. The bandstand pulsed with trumpet

41

heat and slow smoke, and the room was heavy with laughter that didn't quite reach the eyes.

Behind the bar stood Leona Briggs, the club's owner and my sometime informant. She was tall, with cheekbones sharp enough to cut through lies and a voice that could turn sorrow into song. A thousand years ago, when the universe was young, and we were at the University of Michigan, we'd had some unforgettable moments. But our path splintered. For me, the world of writing and broadcast beckoned; for her, it was that world of jazz, blues, and heartache, served up fresh each morning. After some tumultuous years, she found redemption and her true gift—being a successful entrepreneur—when she opened the Blue Lantern some years ago. She was also a powerful behind-the-scenes queen-maker who financed the political campaigns of some of the up-and-coming movers and shakers, most notable, Congressman Charles Diggs, Sr.

"Langston Reed," she said, sliding a glass toward me. "Didn't think you'd show before the weekend. Weren't you writing some fancy radio story?"

"I was," I said, "but the real world wrote something better—and uglier."

I showed her the name on the ledger. "L. C. Whitmore. Ring a bell?"

Leona frowned. "He's been around. Big man in supply for Ford. Plays cards with the wrong kind of people. And there's a white fella he's thick with—name's Reeves, I think. Never seen anyone drink so easy off other folks' sweat."

"Reeves," I repeated. "You sure?"

"Sure as I am about the snow outside."

Leona leaned closer, lowering her voice. "Langston, folks talk. They say some of the parts going missing from the Rouge are being resold downriver, through a warehouse on Jefferson. Government steel, marked as scrap. If Booker knew that, maybe he thought he could stop it."

"And someone decided he couldn't."

She nodded. "Just be careful. The men behind that game don't scare easy."

****

That night, I went to Booker's neighborhood, a maze of row houses squeezed between railroad tracks and smoke. The porch lights were dim, but grief glowed through the cracks like a wound refusing to close.

Elias's brother, Jonah Booker, met me at the door. He was shorter, stockier, and still wore his work clothes—a blue jumpsuit stiff with grease.

"You one of the police?" he asked, guarded.

"No," I said. "A friend of Captain Mercer. I write stories, and sometimes I help him find the truth."

Jonah's eyes softened just enough. "Truth won't bring him back."

"No, but it might keep it from happening again."

He let me in. The house was small, the kind where sorrow has no room to hide. On the mantel was the same photograph I'd found in the locker—Elias's wife and daughter, both now living with her mother down in Toledo.

"He was a good man," Jonah said. "Didn't drink, didn't run around. Just worked hard. He said folks at the plant were cheating the government, and he was gonna tell somebody. I told him to let it go. He said, 'Can't build freedom overseas if we're selling it off at home.' Next night, he was gone."

43

I felt a chill—not from the drafty window, but from the echo of truth. "Did he mention any names?"

"Only one. Reeves. Said the man smiled like a preacher but lied like the devil."

The next day, I went back to Mercer with what I'd learned. He listened, jaw tight, eyes dark with thought.

"Whitmore and Reeves," he said. "We've heard the names, but nobody sticks. War contracts are federal—makes the feds nervous, makes crooks rich."

"You ever think about how many decent men die quiet while the wrong ones get medals?"

"Every damn day," Mercer said.

He pulled on his overcoat. "Come on. There's someone I want you to meet."

We drove down Jefferson Avenue in Mercer's unmarked car, the sound of the police radio interrupting periodically with laconic messages between the dispatcher and scout cars on patrol. We drove past warehouses and shipyards bristling with cranes. The air smelled of iron and gasoline. The sun dipped behind the skyline, and the city turned to silhouette.

Our stop was an old church turned shelter, run by Reverend Amos Caldwell, a soft-spoken preacher who worked with factory men and their families. He'd known Elias Booker.

Caldwell met us at the door, his hands clasped like he was still praying. "Elias came by last week," he said, after we explained. "He wanted to talk about right and wrong. Said his conscience was heavy. I told him truth always costs more than lies, but it's the only currency Heaven takes."

The Reverend led us into the chapel. A single bell hung over the doorway, cracked but proud. "You see that?" he said. "That bell fell during a storm last summer.

Cracked right down the middle. We kept it as a reminder that even broken things can call men to prayer.”

I looked up at it. Something about the way the light hit the bronze made me uneasy. A strange whisper pressed at the back of my mind. Something I couldn’t yet name.

Minutes later, back at Mercer’s car, the dispatcher was frantically calling: “Dispatch to Command 7-Delta.”

Grabbing the mike, Mercer responded quickly, “Command 7-Delta, here.”

“Another body has been found, this time at the old freight yard. Looks like another Rouge worker.”

Mercer cursed softly. “On the way.”

As we left, the Reverend called after us. “Remember, gentlemen—mercy’s easy when it’s late. Harder when it’s due.”

The freight yard sat like a ghost under the moonlight, rails stretching into the distance like forgotten promises. The body lay near a bell-shaped signal post, half-frozen to the ground.

I felt it before I saw it—the same wrongness that had clung to Booker’s death. The same hand behind both.

The tag on the man’s uniform read: L. C. Whitmore.

Mercer crouched beside the corpse. “Well, Langston,” he said quietly, “looks like the man who could’ve explained it all just cashed out early.”

But I wasn’t listening to him. My eyes were on the bell-shaped post, the faint sound it made when the wind cut across it. A hollow, mournful note that seemed to hum through my bones.

In that sound, I heard what my grandmother had called *the whisper*. Not words, not yet. Just a feeling: truth was coming, and it would not come gently.

Ghosts in the Foundry

The morning after Whitmore's body was found, Detroit seemed to wake under a different sky. The smoke over the Rouge plant looked darker, heavier. People still hurried to work, but their eyes stayed low. In wartime, you learned fast how to keep your head down—especially when justice didn't wear your color.

I met Mercer at headquarters. His desk was buried under files, coffee, and the weight of a dozen things he couldn't say out loud.

"Feds are sniffing around," he muttered. "Deputies from Truman's Subcommittee. Looks like the plant is smack dab in the middle of a crucial production schedule. They want to know why a supply supervisor turned up dead when everything's supposed to be running smooth as a new crankshaft."

"Any word on Reeves?"

He shook his head. "Gone. Packed up his room at the Lafayette Hotel last night. Nobody saw him leave."

"Then Whitmore's death wasn't cleanup," I said. "It was insurance. Somebody made sure he couldn't talk."

Mercer's eyes narrowed. "You think Reeves killed him?"

"I think Reeves doesn't get his hands dirty. But someone did."

He tapped his pen on the desk. "I've got men watching the warehouse on Jefferson, but if this thing's half as big as you think, it won't stop there."

I nodded. "Then let's not wait for it to come to us."

By dusk, I was standing outside that warehouse on Jefferson, wrapped in fog and factory noise. Freight trucks came and went, no markings, no paperwork. A single bulb burned over the loading door, yellow and mean.

I slipped through a side entrance, the air thick with oil and rust. Rows of crates lined the floor, stenciled "GOVT PROPERTY—AIRCRAFT SUPPLY." But half of them were empty. Others were filled with cheap scrap—decoys, swapped for real parts already sold to whoever paid best.

Voices echoed from the far end. I moved closer, slow and quiet. Through a crack in the door, I saw two men: one I didn't know, thick and heavyset; the other, unmistakable—Reeves, his hair slick, his suit too clean for honest work.

". . . you shouldn't have killed him here," Reeves was saying. "Whitmore was useful."

The other man shrugged. "He was scared. Started talkin' about goin' to the papers. Couldn't risk it."

Reeves sighed. "War's a fine thing for business—until men grow consciences. We'll move the last shipment tonight. After that, Detroit won't see me again."

I didn't hear the rest because the floorboard under me creaked like a guilty soul. Reeves froze. "Who's there?"

I ran.

Bullets sparked off the steel walls as I dove behind a stack of crates. My heart pounded like a drum line from Paradise Valley. I dashed for the side door, slipped into the night, and didn't stop running until I reached the alley behind St. Philip's Church, three blocks over.

I leaned against the cold brick, gasping, trying to think. The whisper came again—soft, persistent, not in words but in weight. Mercer. Danger. Not alone.

I looked up just in time to see headlights cutting through the fog—a black Packard easing to a stop. Reeves climbed out, cool as a preacher in Sunday whites, revolver glinting in his hand.

He smiled. "Mr. Reed. You should've stuck to your radio shows."

"Those stories pay the rent," I said, keeping my voice steady. "But truth's the one that buys a man peace."

Reeves laughed. "You writers—always mistaking sermons for sense. You think the world's waiting for justice? No, Mr. Reed. The world's waiting for delivery schedules and profit margins."

He raised the gun.

Then, from behind him, a voice cut through the fog. "Drop it, Reeves."

Mercer stepped out from the shadows, revolver steady.

Reeves froze, his smile cracking. "Captain Mercer. I should've guessed."

"Hands up," Mercer said. "It's over."

Reeves's eyes flicked toward me, calculating. I saw the move before he made it—the twitch of the wrist, the flash of metal—and I shouted, "Mercer!"

The shot rang out, but it wasn't Reeves's. Mercer fired once. Reeves staggered back, surprise frozen on his face, then collapsed beside the church steps.

The bell above the church door gave a faint, metallic moan—a ghost note in the night air. I knelt beside the body, not out of pity but because I had to see it through.

Mercer holstered his gun. "You all right?"

"I'll live," I said. "He won't."

Mercer's breath steamed in the cold. "Self-defense," he muttered, as if trying to convince himself. "He went for it."

"He would've killed us both."

"I know." He rubbed his temple. "But it never feels clean, does it?"

I looked at the fallen man, his gun still clutched in his hand. "Nothing worth saving ever is."

****

We called it in, but I stayed behind after the squad car took Reeves's body away. The church bell still swayed in the wind, moaning like a tired ghost. Reverend Caldwell stepped out, eyes gentle but heavy.

"I heard the shot," he said. "Is it finished?"

"Maybe," I said. "But the dirt doesn't stay buried long in this city."

He nodded, then looked at me as if seeing deeper than most ever dared. "You've got a gift, Mr. Reed. Not for words, but for hearing what most men tune out."

"Sometimes I wish I couldn't," I said.

"The Lord doesn't give quiet hearts so they can stay silent," Caldwell said. "You listen, then you speak. That's the work."

His words struck deep. I thought about Booker, about Whitmore, about the men who'd never make headlines but kept the city running. I thought about the way mercy always came too late—like a hand offered after the fall.

When I finally walked home, the streets were empty. My typewriter waited in the dark, keys glinting like old teeth. I sat down and began a new script—not for *The Midnight Detective*, but for myself.

It began, *"In a city of fire and factories, truth walks like a ghost—seen by few, heard by fewer, but never silent."*

I stopped. The whisper came again, faint and steady, like a breath through the rafters. This time, I understood it.

You're not finished yet.

The Quiet Fire

They say Detroit never sleeps—but that's not true. It sleeps in shifts, one man's rest bought by another man's labor. The morning after Reeves went down, I walked those sleeping streets and felt every heartbeat of the city like a low drum underfoot. The war had turned Detroit into an arsenal, but under all that steel and smoke was something older—something trying to wake.

The papers ran the story like they always do: "Local Writer Assists in Capture of Industrial Saboteur." They got my name wrong, called me "Landon Reed." Maybe that was for the best. Fame's a hungry beast; it eats what little peace a man has left.

But peace wasn't what I found when I opened my door that morning.

A letter lay on my table—no address, no stamp. Just my name, written in the careful hand of a man with something to hide.

Inside was a single sheet: *You don't know the whole of it. Meet me at the River Rouge foundry, midnight.—W.*

Whitmore was dead. Reeves was dead. But that initial still carried weight like a gravestone. I folded the letter, tucked it in my coat, and waited for the dark.

The foundry was a cathedral of fire and shadow, roaring with machines and molten light. Sparks rose to the ceiling like prayers no one answered. Midnight hit, and with it came a figure stepping out from behind the furnace glow.

It wasn't Whitmore. It was Booker Johnson, my friend from the bar, his eyes hard and tired.

"Booker," I said. "You're supposed to be working nights at Packard."

He shook his head. "Ain't been there in weeks. Not since they found out I knew too much."

"About Reeves?"

"About who was paying Reeves," he said quietly. "This wasn't just a black-market scheme. These contracts were feeding a bigger machine—one that don't care what side wins, long as the money flows."

He handed me a folder, smudged with grease. Inside were invoices, coded telegrams, and one name that chilled the air between us: Alden Manufacturing. That was Whitmore's employer—and a top supplier for the Army Air Corps.

Booker said, "they been sellin' counterfeit engine parts to both sides, Langston. Half of what's in them crates can't fly ten miles without failin'. The Army knows, but they don't care—they just need numbers, not souls."

The roar of the foundry filled the silence. The truth felt too big for words.

Then came footsteps—Mercer's voice cutting through the steam. "Reed! You here?"

Booker froze. "You brought him?"

"I didn't," I said. "He must've followed me."

Mercer stepped into the light, coat unbuttoned, hand near his holster. "Put it down, Booker. Whatever that folder is, it's evidence."

Booker's jaw tightened. "Evidence for who, Captain? I hand this over, it disappears. Men like Reeves ain't the top of this ladder—they're just the rungs."

"Booker," I said, "listen to me. This isn't just about the truth. It's about staying alive long enough to tell it."

But Booker's eyes were wild with something past fear—that quiet rage that builds when you've been good too long in a bad world. "You think the truth lives in paper, Langston? No. It lives in blood."

He reached for something in his coat—not a gun, but a matchbook. Before I could stop him, he struck one and tossed it into a pool of oil. Flame roared to life, licking up the walls, swallowing the noise of reason.

Mercer lunged forward, grabbed Booker's arm. They struggled—a dance of desperation in orange light—until Booker slipped, fell hard. The fire caught fast, crackling like laughter. Mercer shouted for me to help, but Booker was gone before I reached him, swallowed by smoke.

We barely made it out.

Outside, the sirens howled, the foundry's skeleton glowing like a dying sun behind us. Mercer leaned against his car, face smeared with soot and sorrow. "He was right, you know," he said quietly. "We'll never get them all."

"No," I said, watching sparks rise into the night. "But we can make them nervous."

He looked at me, eyes red. "You gonna print what you found?"

"Not in the papers. Too easy to bury. But I'll write it the only way I can."

Mercer nodded, then climbed into his car and drove off. I stood there a while longer, the smoke settling over me like the weight of the city itself.

* * * *

Back home, the typewriter waited. I fed in a fresh page and began again.

This is the story of men who make fire and call it light, of hands that build wings but never fly. This is Detroit, 1942—where mercy walks the midnight streets, looking for someone still listening.

I paused. The whisper came again, not from heaven or conscience but from somewhere deep—that intuitive fire I'd carried since childhood, when my grandmother told me the Lord sometimes speaks between the beats of your heart.

I heard her voice now, soft and steady: *"Use it, Langston. Don't waste what you've been given."*

So I wrote.

I wrote until dawn broke over the rooftops, painting the city gold. I wrote about men who steal in the name of progress, about others who die trying to stop them, and about the thin, stubborn hope that mercy—even midnight mercy—might one day come before judgment.

When I finished, I tore the last page from the typewriter and set it aside. Outside, the factory whistles began their morning song. Somewhere, a church bell answered.

I stood at the window and whispered a prayer that wasn't quite a prayer—more a promise. To keep listening. To keep writing. To keep mercy alive, even in the darkest hours.

Because in a city like this, that's the only way truth survives.

53

AI Disclosure for this story: AI was used in the early ideation and research process, and in the early editing and proofreading process.

The Thing in the Mirror

By Abel Ramirez

Sketchpad in hand, Roland strolled into Colombo's 24-hour diner on Main Street in downtown Ravensblood. He didn't care that it was nearly two-thirty in the morning. He'd lived in town for years, and he walked the streets however late he damn well pleased. But now the arthritis in his hip impeded his gait as he made his way to his usual booth by the front window, which looked out on Main and the row of shops lining it. He ordered his usual coffee with cream and three sugars.

The diner was redolent of eggs and coffee. Even though the Michigan state law prohibiting smoking in public places had gone into effect years ago, a faint scent of nicotine still lingered. Leon, the cook, had probably lit one up in the back before Roland walked in. Mona, a heavyset server dressed in her customary black pants, black top, and beaten-up sneakers, served Roland a cup of piping-hot coffee.

"Anything else, Roland?" she asked, popping a stick of gum into her mouth.

Roland chuckled. The question was rhetorical, they both knew. He'd been coming here to work for decades, and she'd been serving here just as long. When he came at this time of night, he only ever ordered coffee. If he stayed until sunup, he would leave with a Danish to go.

When Mona ambled away, Roland took a sip from his cup, watching his image reflected in the large window beside him facing Main Street. He thought about time and its passage. *Time is the fire in which we all burn,* he thought. He no longer had jet-black hair and smooth skin. Now, he was in his seventies, and his remaining wisps of white hair were neatly combed to the side. Deep lines and wrinkles adorned his face like a spider's web.

Opening his sketchpad he looked over his latest drawing—a striking woman in her mid to late twenties looked back at him. He stared at her, pleased that he'd captured Vivian's likeness from memory, even after all these years. He thought of his youth, of a blazing summer afternoon at the old Tiger Stadium on Michigan Avenue and Rosa Parks Boulevard, before it was torn down. That was where he first laid eyes on her beautiful face.

Vivian was there with her family, standing in front of him in line at the hot dog stand. He was smitten at the sight of her and struck up a conversation. They kept in touch after the game and soon the two were inseparable. A few months later, when Vivian and her family moved to Ravensblood, a small town north of Detroit, Roland packed up and moved to find work—whatever he could get—just so he could be close to her.

Roland removed a pencil from his shirt pocket and began working on the final touches to his piece. As he finished shading the corner of an eye, he suddenly sat upright. He felt as if an icy hand had reached out to touch him, from a grave closed so long ago. A chill spread to the very core of his soul.

He looked up, scanning the room. It was unusually empty. Even this time of night, Colombo's usually had a few stragglers—night owls, insomniacs, cops, or truck drivers. Not tonight; save for Mona and Leon, the place was vacant.

That early in the morning, the streets of Ravensblood were just as barren. Few headlights were in motion, even fewer pedestrians—only the endless dark of night, which now seemed darker with the broken streetlight out front. A lonely gloom filled the atmosphere. It made Roland feel uneasy, and restlessness.

Just then, the bell connected to the front door rang out, overly loud in the bludgeoning silence. Startled, Roland looked up from his sketchpad to see Jack, another regular, saunter into the diner. He, like Roland, was another senior citizen, though younger than Roland by almost a decade. Jack waved to Roland and began weaving his way toward him, to the booth by the window. On the way, he exchanged pleasantries with Mona and ordered coffee— cream, no sugar.

A stout man with a gray pompadour and sideburns, Jack had some trouble squeezing into the booth opposite Roland. His beer-and-burger belly pressed against the edge of the table as he scooted into place with a grunt, the effort reflected on his face.

Roland frowned. Something about Jack that night caused Roland to feel unsettled.

"You okay, Ro? You're looking at me like you've never seen me before."

Mona came by and set Jack's coffee on the table. "Thanks, dear," he said in his gravelly tone. Years of smoking had given him his distinctive growl.

"Anything else?" she asked.

"Yeah," Jack said. "How about a patty melt and chili-cheese fries? Extra cheese."

"Sure thing, honey," Mona said, already walking away.

Jack turned back to Roland.

"Whaddya say, Roland?" Jack said, still struggling to get comfortable. "You look a little pale. Are you all right?"

"Just a little gloomy in here tonight is all," Roland

replied, his voice taut. He quickly closed his sketchpad.

"Does seem kind of dismal in here . . . " Jack said, inspecting the diner. "Well, whatever it is, don't let it get you down."

At that moment, the bell on the front door jingled again, and the muscles in Roland's neck knotted when he saw who entered. Sal Wallace, a local private detective, stepped inside in a gray trench coat, a matching fedora fixed crookedly on his head. Under his coat, he wore a rumpled blue suit and tie, the latter loosened, with the top buttons of his white dress shirt undone. Sal was still in good shape for a man in his late sixties—he had to be, making his living tracking down and filming people engaged in illicit affairs.

Sal stepped up to the counter, sat on a stool, and asked for a black coffee, his trench coat hanging down. Roland and Jack glared at him the entire time—especially Roland.

"Try not to think about him," Jack whispered. "It was forty years ago. A whole lifetime has gone by."

"I let it go a long, long time ago," Roland replied, matching Jack's whisper, his eyes narrowing at Sal. "But all said and done, I can never forget."

Mona handed Sal his black coffee in a white Styrofoam cup. The private eye paid, got up, then glanced in Roland's direction. Roland saw a flicker of recognition on his otherwise stoic, granite face before he exited the diner.

"Every time I see him," Roland said, raising his voice now that Sal was gone. "I always think of him with Vivian. How ironic. Now he catches other people messing around for a living." He gazed into the dark recesses of his coffee cup.

"You're a strong man, Roland. I don't know what I would've done if I'd found my wife in bed with another man. I still want to kill my asshole boss for firing me last week. He knows I don't have enough to retire. I gave thirty years of my life to that damn company. And what do I get for all my years of service? The middle finger!"

Roland had heard the story of Andy firing Jack so many times over the past five days that at this point he could tell it himself. Truth be told, it was Jack's own fault for showing up late and hungover one too many times. Andy had given him plenty of chances. Roland just wanted Jack to stop talking about it; he was sick of the whole thing. He was about to say something—anything—to change the subject, but when he glanced up at Jack, Roland froze. He took deep breaths and beads of sweat began to glisten on his forehead.

Jack stopped ranting before he could really start, and his tone shifted from righteous indignation to concern.

"What's wrong, buddy? You don't look so good." Jack reached over to Roland, who was rubbing his left tear duct with his pinky finger.

"Yeah, I'm fine," Roland sighed shakily. "Just got something in my eye." He sipped his coffee. "Jack, I gotta tell you something. It's important—something I've kept secret for forty years now. Something I ain't never told no one else."

Jack leaned in, his expression serious.

"What is it, Roland?"

"I ain't as strong as you think I am. I almost did it," Roland said in a conspiratorial whisper.

"Did what?"

"I almost killed Vivian and Sal the night I caught them together."

"Are you serious?" Jack practically shouted.

"Keep your voice down," Roland snapped, glancing at Mona and Leon, who were minding their own business.

"You almost offed Vivian and Sal?" Jack said in whisper.

"I came close. When Viv and I got married and moved in together over on Wilbur Street, my Uncle George gave me a pistol. To protect my new wife and our home, you know. To keep the family we were about to start safe. It was Smith & Wesson six-shot revolver."

Roland took a sip of coffee, then continued.

"It wasn't long before I learned about Vivian and Sal. Just a few months, really. The signs were there, like how Viv would always work late at the furniture factory. She had the afternoon shift but sometimes wouldn't come home till one in the morning. It didn't sit right with me. I didn't know exactly what was going on until I decided to find out for myself. One night, I parked down the block from where she worked and waited to see what time she left."

Roland took another sip of coffee. He paused, savoring the taste, leaving Jack in suspense.

"Go on," Jack encouraged.

"Vivian left the factory at ten p.m., long before she told me she'd be out. She got into the white Plymouth her parents bought her, and I followed. At first, I thought she saw me trailing her, but she didn't. I stayed a good distance behind as she drove to the Lamplighter Motel. Remember that dive?"

Jack nodded. "Parts of it were torn down and rebuilt, but it's still there."

"Yeah, on 35th Street. Anyhow, she pulled up to the building and parked next to a blue Chrysler sitting in front of Room 114."

Roland's rheumy eyes filmed over, taking on a faraway look as he relived the trauma for what felt like the hundredth—no, the thousandth time. The years had dulled the sharp edge of the memory, but it still hurt.

"Sal opened the door of the motel room. It was the first time I saw his ruddy face. Vivian kissed him on the mouth, then waltzed right in and closed the door behind her."

Roland took a deep breath.

"My heart dropped, Jack. It fell a thousand feet into a pit. All I could feel was jealousy . . . and anger. I couldn't take it. I turned around and went home for the pistol meant to protect her." He smirked wistfully at the irony. "I was gonna use it to kill Vivian and the man she was screwing."

Fountains of emotion sprang up from Roland's chest, rooted in memory. He sniffed, then took a deep breath, trying to steady himself.

"When I came back to the Lamplighter with the gun, Sal was just leaving. He got into his car and drove off. Vivian's Plymouth was still there, so I knew she was still inside."

Roland opened his sketchpad, turned to a blank page, and started drawing frantically. The harsh sound of the pencil scratching against the paper seemed loud in the nearly deserted diner.

"As soon as Sal was gone, I parked in his spot," Roland explained, still sketching. "I knocked on their door. My hand grasped the gun so hard my knuckles turned white. Even though I loved her, all I could think about was what she'd done with him and what I was going to do. I was driven by pure hatred and rage."

"'Back so soon, honey?' Viv says from inside. 'Did

you forget something?' She opened the door wearing a red silk nightie, finding the barrel of the Smith & Wesson pointed at her pretty face. Her long blonde hair was disheveled after her romp in the sack. I pushed my way in, slamming the door behind me. Vivian tried to scream, but she could only gasp instead. She took a couple of steps backward toward the bed with its soiled sheets."

"'Yes, honey, back so soon,' I tell her. 'How could you do this, Viv? How could you?'" Roland's sketching motions accelerated, the pencil racing across the paper almost of its own volition.

"'Roland . . . Roland, please stop. Don't do this. Don't let it make you do this.' When she said those words, she didn't look at me. Her eyes were fixed on something behind me instead."

"'Don't let *it* make you do this?'" Jack echoed. "Was she talking about your anger making you do it? Your rage?"

"No. She was talking about some *thing* else."

"What do you mean?"

"She told me she saw something that night. She called it a monster." He was drawing impossibly fast now.

"She saw a monster? Do you mean you, Roland? Because of what you were gonna do?"

"No. Not me. 'It's standing right behind you,' Vivian kept saying. She didn't scream. She just stood there, transfixed, mouth hanging open, with an expression of horror on her face. It was that look of terror that made me look over my shoulder, but I saw nothing there. I looked back at Viv. I aimed the gun at her face, and I was about to pull the trigger."

Jack listened, rapt, his eyes widening.

"But when I took another step toward her, I noticed the mirror above the dresser to my right . . . I looked into it

. . . and I saw it, Jack. The thing behind me . . . just like Viv said. It was standing right behind me the entire time, only I couldn't see the damn thing when I looked over my shoulder—but *she* could."

Mona came by and set Jack's food on the table, but he was oblivious to it. She topped off both of their cups. Roland nodded his thanks and didn't resume speaking until she was out of earshot. Not once did his drawing hand waver.

"It stood there behind me with its arm stretched forward, alongside my arm. Its hand clutching my hand, guiding me, holding the revolver with me, pushing me, prompting me to murder her. It used my rage and jealousy, pushing me to pull the trigger and splatter Viv's brains all over the room. I was going to do it, too—until I saw it."

Roland finished his drawing, turned the sketchpad over, but didn't put down his pencil.

"I saw its gnarled body and twisted face in the mirror, Jack. It turned its head and looked straight at me through the glass."

Roland snapped the pencil in two. He was holding it that tight. He turned the sketchpad over and looked at his work, keeping it away from Jack.

"You've got to be kidding me, Roland."

"No. I'm not. When I saw the thing, I knew what it was trying to do. It was urging me to kill them both—and then myself. But when I saw it, I couldn't go through with it, Jack. I ran right out of the Lamplighter and didn't look back. I don't know if she ever told Sal what happened that night. I divorced Vivian and tried to forget it all. But every time I see Sal, I'm reminded of that thing in the mirror."

"I bet," Jack said, looking horrified. "I've never heard anything like that before."

Finally, Roland turned the sketchpad to Jack. "This is what it looked like."

The face in the drawing, if you could call it a face, was the stuff of nightmares—an indescribable horror with vacant eyes. It was just a drawing, but it seemed to be looking right through Jack. He grimaced and turned away.

"Jack," Roland began. "I need to ask something of you."

"Yeah," Jack said, with effort. "What is it?"

"I know you have something planned tonight. Something bad. Don't do it. Just let it go."

"Let what go?" Jack said, alarmed. "What are you talking about, Roland?"

"Don't play coy with me, Jack. I know what you're planning to do to Andy for firing you. Look in the window's reflection, Jack. It's standing right behind you."

The Stream

by Marsalis Higgs

Did you hear about the girl who died on the stream?

It happened a long time ago, sometime in the 22nd century.

She was a nice girl. Sweet, kind, considerate. She got good grades, kept to herself. But that didn't mean much to the circle of girls who ruled the school.

They were jealous of how much the teachers adored her. They were jealous of how much the boys looked her way. They were jealous of how much she seemed not to truly care about what others thought.

And that was why they had to break her.

They began with her locker. Stuffing it with dead rats and dead bugs. They put a rotted fish head in her lunch bag. They broke the screen of her classroom tablet. They poured water over the stall when she sat down to use the bathroom.

They called her names. Followed her down the hall and jeered at her. They spread rumors about her family, the way she smelled, how she had to take the hyper-rail to school from her dingy, dirty neighborhood near all the abandoned factories.

They made sure she was not invited to parties at the hover park. They made sure she was not invited to the mega mall. They made sure that she was not invited to trips to the moon, or to Mars.

And little by little, they did break her. She stopped smiling, stopped talking. She stopped doing her homework. She stopped even going to school.

But the girls still kept going. It was on that old app, BlokParty, where the most damage was done.

They made fake accounts and sent her obscene messages. Sent disgusting pictures, videos of murders and accidents and executions. They'd pretend to be boys wanting to date her, only to later reveal themselves as the monsters they were. They threatened her life. They told her she should do it, she should just end it.

That's when she turned on her livestream and looked into the camera and she knew all of them were watching, and she did it. But before she did, she made a vow to herself that it would not end there—there would be more to come, and she meant what she said.

Because shortly thereafter, each of the girls who had picked on her began to experience funny things happening to them.

One of the girls, after yelling at her butler bot for putting her clothing in the wrong drawer, was herself grabbed by the butler and stuffed into the drawer so harshly that her neck broke instantly.

And another girl was getting a routine manicure when the manicure bot slashed through her fingers, and then through her hands, chopping them both off at the wrists.

Another girl was being driven by her car down the freeway when the autopilot malfunctioned and ran her into the Detroit River.

Another girl was taking a trip with her family to Mercury when her spacesuit began to leak, and her skin was boiled to a crisp.

And the last girl, oh the last one, was on her tablet when she found a video of a girl who looked just like herself. Watching the video, she noticed a shadowy figure behind the girl. And the figure came from behind the girl and grabbed the girl's neck, and she struggled and struggled but could not get away. And then the girl lay there with her eyes open, dead.

And that's when the girl threw her tablet and turned around and there was the girl who'd died on the live stream. And she smiled and reached out her hands for the girl's neck.

And they found her like that, on the floor of her bedroom, with her eyes open, and dark handprints across her neck.

And to this day, they say that anyone who watches that video will be met by the girl who died on the stream.

At least, that's what they say.

The Witch

By Keith A. Owens

I See You

The first time I saw her, she was homeless. At least that's how she looked to me. Face like a rat, ink-black hair streaked with silver, matted up in greasy clumps, wearing a filthy oversized coat that covered a threadbare red dress and several more mismatched layers of clothing. Plus, she was pushing a grocery cart full of large black plastic bags and other belongings, which is standard for homeless folk. Or I guess the new and more politically correct term is 'un-housed', right? Personally, I don't see the damned difference, and I don't see how being *unhoused* makes your life better than if you're *homeless*; if you're un-*housed* then your ass is home*less*.

But whatever. It's a gripe of mine, and I have more than a few. The point is the woman fit the description for being homeless here in Detroit, or pretty much anywhere else. You see them and you forget them, which may be the sad truth, but it's the truth. As I was about to pass by her on the street—I was taking a lunch break from where I work downtown—she was shambling along in that jerky rhythm so many of them do, talking to herself and grinning like a Halloween pumpkin. Subconsciously, I'm sure my mind was already preparing to erase her existence from my memory banks before that pitiful existence ever had a chance to register.

I got close enough to become annoyed by the squeaky wheels on her cart, and also to have my nostrils violated by her unpleasantness. Her unwashed funk, which was amplified by the heat and humidity of mid-summer when the smells of the city announce themselves at every turn, was like an assault. I squinted, coughed, and turned my head to the side. I held my breath and picked up my pace, hoping that would get me upwind of the woman's unusually foul odor. That's when she took a sudden, deliberate step in my direction. The rapid, unexpected motion drew my attention to her face, and that's when I noticed her eyes were spinning like pinwheels. I made a motion to jump back, but she reached out and grabbed my arm with a vice grip that could have crushed cement.

She was smiling, but the smile was gentle. Nothing like the jack-o'-lantern expression she wore a few minutes ago. The warmth on her face, which contrasted so sharply with everything else, threw me off and made me confused.

"I see you," she said, her voice sounding like a paper bag full of whispers.

I tried to snatch my arm away, but that only added an exclamation point to the pain as she squeezed harder while her nails dug into the fabric of my sportscoat. I glanced down as a reflex to see what the hell kind of nails this woman had, and they didn't look like anything that should belong on a human being. They were filthy, caked with what I thought was dirt but could have been something else, and they were at least an inch long. And they didn't extend from the top of her fingers like what you see on folks. Instead, each finger and her thumb transformed from mottled brown flesh into a hard, sharpened claw.

"I see you, Marcellus James."

This time it was my mother's voice. . .

A Momma's Boy

When I was a kid growing up on the west side of the city, my mother and I, we were really close. My Dad had passed away before I was able to form any memories of him, although there were pictures of his smiling, dark chocolate face all around the house. Always some expression of joy. My favorite caught him laughing at what had to have been the funniest thing he ever heard, his mouth wide, exposing a mouth full of beautiful white teeth. His head was tilted back, his eyes squeezed shut to where small stress lines stretched out from the corners.

"That one was taken all the way out in Aspen, Colorado, when we were with him at that conference. You probably don't remember because you were just a baby back then," she told me once when she noticed me staring at it on the mantle above the fireplace.

Mom told me she never wanted another man after my dad because "there isn't a man alive who could ever measure up, so it just wouldn't be fair." My mother was fair-skinned with reddish hair and freckles and let's just say a full-figured Black woman's body that left no doubt. I witnessed more than one poor guy thinking maybe he had cracked the code that would at least get him under those sheets if not into her heart. But Mom was a master at letting men down easy with that seductive smile and those greenish eyes while somehow managing to steer them away without bruising their pride—and before they tried to make her pay a price once they realized she was turning them down.

"Because that's the way most men are," she told me once. "They wanna make the woman pay for something that they tryin' to steal. You hear what I'm saying? Not pay for; *steal.* Not your father, though. He was something special."

I was about 12, maybe 13, when she said that. We were sitting outside on the front porch as we liked to do sometimes once the weather got nice and we could just talk. It was a nice quiet block where we lived, one where the neighbors waved at you and the kids enjoyed speeding up and down the street without fear of any wild car screeching around the corner promising a threat to their joy.

That's the thing I'll always remember and love the most about my mother, how we would always talk—not like a mother giving her child instruction but just one human being who especially enjoyed talking to and sharing things with another. It always made me feel like she didn't just love me, like parents were supposed to do as part of the contract, but that she actually liked and respected me too. And sometimes, just to emphasize that point, when our conversation was coming to a close and we were ready to go back inside, Mom would lean over and squeeze me on the knee before giving me a light kiss on the cheek and then whispering in my ear. . .

"I see you, Marcellus James."

It's What Witches Do

"What's that you said?"

The woman gave me a mock questioning look, almost like a clown's mask with an upside-down frown painted across the bottom of her face. She shook her head, pretending she didn't understand the question. This time, maybe because my anger was fueling my adrenaline, I managed to snatch my arm free of her grasp as I took a couple steps back.

"You called my name. You said, 'I see you'. That's what. . . how do you know my damned name? *How do you know my name?*"

The frown stretched slowly upward into a grotesque parody of a smile where the corners of her mouth were now so high it was a freakish, near-impossible achievement that made me want to scream. It was no longer gentle. Her teeth, like her nails, were thick, dirty, and sharp, and a thick blackish tongue snaked around behind them inside her mouth as if preparing to strike.

I felt like there was nothing else in existence beyond the whisper-thin membrane that had wrapped itself around us like a tent. We were sizing each other up inside this soundless, invisible bubble that managed to shield our interactions from the busyness of the lunchtime masses scurrying by on Woodward. Most of them were deeply absorbed into their own don't-bother-me world of phones and ear pods, sharing conversation with other remote someones moving about inside bubbles of their own. It made me wonder if this contraption was even necessary to keep us hidden from sight. These days it seemed we were all hidden from each other's sight by design.

But whatever.

"It's what witches do," the woman said, her voice now sounding scratchy and rough, not at all like my mother's.

Then she slowly raised one leg to where it appeared she was balancing herself on the other like a stork, that horrible grin fixed in place as if it had been stapled there. Effortlessly, she raised the other leg as well so that both knees were pulled up to her chest as she remained suspended in mid-air. Her arms were outstretched, the clawed fingers of both hands pointing downward, making her resemble a huge bird of prey. Next, she folded her legs to where it looked as if she was seated on a bench—except there was no bench.

I was numb. I suspect my brain didn't know any other way to protect itself—and the rest of me—from shutting down and checking out. Initially, there was a rapid, scattered attempt to flip through any and all rational explanations—again, a form of self-protection—but too soon it became apparent that whatever was rational wouldn't do me any good right now. Because whatever this was, it was happening in real time right in front of me, and I was going to have to deal with it on its own terms.

"Witch. . . ?" I said, my voice feeling dry, but sounding as if there was a bit of an echo.

The woman nodded slowly.

Yes, dear heart.

This time her response was mainlined straight through my skull to an internal receptor I didn't even know was there. I wondered if maybe this was one of those leftover parts of the body from several evolutions ago, like the gill slits they say you can see in embryos, but then something else in me said I read way too much science fiction.

But this isn't science fiction, is it dear heart?

Her grotesquely distorted lips hadn't moved at all, but the flickering amusement in her eyes seemed to be taking pleasure in my shocked reaction. Her body, which had been encased in rags and ruin, now appeared to be shapeshifting between the dual appearances of smoke and liquid.

"This is real, Marcellus."

My mother's voice again. I felt anger boiling up to overtake my fear and shock.

"Is there a reason why you're using my mother's voice? Because I don't think that's necessary. Whatever it is you're trying to do here, why you had to pick me for whatever it is you have in mind, I don't see any reason why you had to drag my mother into this. She's been dead for. . ."

"Nine years, isn't it? Yes. April 23, 2016. Only 69 years of age when she just seemed to crumple and fold, like a balled-up brown paper bag. She was taking a rest on that exquisite brown leather couch, wasn't she? The one she had just bought the week before."

Here, the witch's wrecked face took solid form in the midst of the swirl. It was a mocking joke of a sad clown mask that looked. . . Jesus. It looked like my mother. I wanted to kill her.

"And *you*. Only 24 years old and just getting a foothold on your new life. Such a shame how that had to happen, how such a beautiful woman like that can seem to give up on life all of a sudden for no reason at all. Because we both know Donatella James was far too young to have left you so soon. But we do adapt to life's challenges, don't we? Just look at *you!*"

Her voice was no longer raping the insides of my skull, but having this thing toy with me using Mom's voice was far worse. I resisted the urge to lunge at the swirling mass of flesh and fluid because I figured that's what she wanted. Also because I could hear the memory of my real mother's voice warning me against making a decision that could get me killed—or worse. I had never considered the possibility that there could be much of anything worse than death, but as I experienced this surreal scenario taking place during what was supposed to be my lunch break, it occurred to me that death might be far preferable to whatever kind of eternal pain this thing might have the power to inflict.

"Yeah. Just look at me," I said sarcastically. "Who could ask for anything more than where I am right now?

"*You* could, Marcellus. That's who. You could ask for anything you want, dear heart."

Again, I almost made a wrong decision, and again, the warmth of my mother's spirit urged me to take a step back from doing something stupid.

A moment later I smiled, which provoked a corresponding moment of discomfort I sensed coming from the witch, like maybe she was caught off guard. Her form, which had been shifting in and out of shapes like a molten mass, paused its restlessness. Eventually, it settled on the more solid appearance of a nightmare creature possessing the large head of a raven (replacing the sad clown mask), but still attached to the body of the pathetic homeless woman I had seen not even an hour ago. Slowly, her stockinged legs unfolded from mid-air and lowered themselves to the ground as the raven's gaze, electric in its intensity, remained fixed on me.

"You are amused, I see," she said.

I shook my head.

"Not a damned thing amusing about any of this, and if you had any idea of what it must feel like to be me right now, then you'd know this wasn't what I had in mind when I decided to leave my office and go to lunch. All I fucking wanted was *lunch,* OK?"

Maybe this wasn't the time to be getting snippy, but it was either taking a chance on the false bravado or falling to the ground and bawling like a little kid. I had no idea whether all those folks walking to and fro past the bubble I shared with the witch could see what was going on and were choosing to ignore it, or whether we really were invisible to them. But if they could actually see me? Well. That just wasn't gonna work because word gets around.

"You are amused," she said again, taking a step closer. My stolen mother's voice this time sounded tinny and a bit metallic, like it was being filtered through a can.

I started to say something, but the raven's head hissed. The black eyes smoldered.

"You asked a question. About your mother. About why I took her voice. But I am surprised you didn't think to ask how it is that I know the voice of Donatella James at all. Because shouldn't that be the question you're asking? How it is that I know so much about your mother? And then you may want to ask the question whether this old witch knows things about your mother that you never did."

My anger started boiling again.

"I said you need to leave my mother out of this," I said quietly, which was how I spoke when I felt like I was about to blow.

"And now your fake amusement has given way to the reality of your anger, and that is because you sense that a certain truth is cutting too close."

"What the hell would a witch know about any kind of truth?"

The head of the raven morphed into the head of a grinning black cat with emerald eyes. One of them winked at me.

"Oh dear heart. The truth is what witches do."

Donatella

There was nothing about Donatella as a child that gave even a hint of whose child she was, or who she might become once she had left her painful childhood behind. She was a small-boned, coffee-and-cream-colored Black girl who was forced to wear comically large black-frame glasses so that she could bear witness to the doings of a world in which she had very little interest.

No, that's not quite right. Actually, Donatella was *very* interested in the world around her, just not the world that was *immediately* around her. Because the sordid details of *that* particular world were the sort that placed her inside an off-balance picture frame containing a drunken mother and happy-go-lucky father whose moods traveled back and forth between the seasons at whim, sometimes within the confines of a single day—or even hour. Which meant that one minute Ellis James could be whistling a favorite tune as he stood in front of the stove in their tiny apartment, making his baby girl's favorite blueberry pancakes, but then the weather would change somewhere between the preparation of pancakes and the anticipated delivery to the breakfast table. The clouds would gather as her father's abnormally deep voice (for someone so small in stature because for goodness' sake the man was barely just creeping above five foot tall and there were large dogs who weighed more than him) would gather thunder to match the lightning that sparked in his eyes as he threw the griddle with half-made pancakes through the kitchen into the wall of the living room, narrowly missing the head of Fantasma James, his wife, adorned with the ever-present pink and blue rollers in her hair, hanging at odd lengths and angles making her look like a confused rag doll. She was slouched to the side just out of aim on the sofa, smoking a cigarette while pretending to watch TV.

"Why ain't *you* the one making these damned pancakes for your daughter, Fan? Ain't you the mother? *Ain't you?* Ain't that what mothers supposed to do is make breakfast for they children?"

Which was when Fan, who Donatella had always assumed was her mother, simply shrugged her amused indifference, not missing a line of dialogue of whatever happened to be on screen at the time, except to say "but they gotta be your children first, nigguh."

"You shut your damned mouth, Fan! *You shut your damned mouth!*"

Which was when Donatella, who only happened to be eight years old at the time—old enough to catch the gist of what she had just heard—scooted around from her seat at the breakfast table where she had been waiting for pancakes to focus her oversized black frames on thought-you-were-my-mother.

"Momma. . . what. . . ?"

Which was when Fan began to slowly crouch and sink into the cushions, afraid to meet the inquiring gaze of an 8-year-old child who should never have had to ask that question.

"It ain't nothin' baby," she muttered. "It ain't nothin'. Your Momma and Daddy just fightin' is all. You know how we fight. This ain't the first time you. . . "

"But Momma you said. . . "

"Donnie don't you worry 'bout what your mother said, hear?" said her father, whose volcanic mood had suddenly shifted to another much more comfortable season. "Daddy's gonna make you some more pancakes.

OK? Daddy's gonna make you some *more* pancakes. With *lotsa* blueberries, OK? Big fat ones too! Just how you like."

"But Momma said. . . "

There was the sound of a bowl crashing and tinkling as it exploded against the floor. Almost like it was screaming. Donatella had always liked that bowl for some reason, the pretty red, yellow and green swirling designs of smiling small animals that had been painted along the sides. It had been a large mixing bowl, not the kind of dish any child would normally pay attention to, but to Donatella— 'Donnie' as her father sometimes liked to call her—it just *looked* like something that had been made especially for her. And since she didn't have many things, certainly not many toys or dolls (she had lots of promises though, of all the wonderful things Mommy and Daddy were *going to* get for her but then there would always be another *something* standing guard, mocking her, between the promise and the delivery), then her very special bowl that her parents never quite understood was special (because why would a bowl be special to a child?) began to fulfill the promise of all those other barren promises that Donnie began to understand would never be allowed to breathe.

But now the shattered bowl lay in sharp-edged pieces all over the kitchen floor in sharp edges. For a painfully extended moment the apartment grew silent as the echo of her father's inexplicable rage faded into empty. Fantasma straightened her posture on the couch to where she nearly resembled who she had once been as a young woman and shot Ellis a look meant to kill, but Ellis never saw the look. Only felt it as he stood quietly at the stove looking down at the bits and pieces of his worthless anger. As for Donatella, a small tear leaked from the corner of her left eye.

"You broke my bowl, daddy," she whimpered.

Ellis didn't even bother to contest the small child's misplaced claim to ownership of a dish that should have been a toy as he tried to ignore the scratching accusation inside his brain of who he was not and would never be. But what he could not ignore was the way his small daughter sucked in an impossibly large breath that never could have found space inside a child's lungs. Except that anger always finds its way somehow. Anger always makes its room.

"You broke my bowl, daddy!" the child screeched at an unholy volume that shook the entire apartment building to where doors were timidly opened up and down the hallway as neighbors peeked out and regarded one another with expressions of fear and questioning.

But none of those expressions could match the level of fear that had now taken up residence inside the home of the James family. Well, maybe just in Ellis, who stared wide-eyed at his only child as an unrecognizable horror that had somehow invaded his home. His hands hung limply by his sides, fingers fidgeting as he began to tremble. His mouth opened to speak, but there were no words, only a dry whispering of air that spilled out.

Fantasma, however, was smiling. Like a proud mother whose little girl finally delivered the performance of a lifetime at the school recital. She was no longer slouching but sitting up straight as could be on the couch, leaning forward slightly as if in anticipation of whatever was coming next. Her bird-like hands were folded in her lap, her dark brown eyes sparkling. And when *she* opened her mouth, the words were not afraid to come out.

"You know what, little girl? I think you might just be mine for real after all. Come on over here, baby."

Donatella Makes A Friend

But Donatella did not want to come over there. She could smell the lie in her mother's words almost as well as she could smell the desperation. What kind of mother would have felt drawn closer to her child after an outburst like that? What kind of mother warms herself beside the heated confusion of her own child?

Someone who was not really her mother, who was just pretending. But why?

"I need to go out," she said quietly, still sitting awkwardly in her chair as her father's mouth continued to move soundlessly. Fantasma leaned forward with her arms outstretched, a twisted smile pulled across her face, as if she hadn't heard.

"Come on over here, baby," she said again, this time her voice taking on a bit more urgency. "Momma needs to talk to you. There are things. . . "

"I need to go outside. Please. You need to let me go outside."

Fantasma's rubber smile began to contort out of true, but her arms remained outstretched, not so much welcoming but reaching. And there was a difference.

"Baby, why you think you need to go outside right now? Besides, you too young to go out there all by yourself, and you too little. You got to be grown like your daddy and me to just walk yourself up and down the street, girl. You ain't nothin' but a child, so why don't you. . . "

"Let the girl go, Fan."

Fantasma's eyes caught fire in their sockets as she rose from her faux mothering position on the couch, both hands firming themselves into hardened balls of flesh and bone as they planted one on each hip. Then her neck began to work.

"Ellis James? Lemme tell you somethin', and you better hear me the first time 'cause if there gotta be a next time then I can promise it ain't gonna be any kinda time you will appreciate, hear me?"

Ellis was no longer regarding his daughter with horror, or even paying her much attention. Instead, he had resumed the uncomfortably familiar posture of confrontation with his wife that had become standard procedure several times a week for the past three years of their marriage ever since their son—Ellis Jr., Donatella's baby brother—had died in his crib early on a Saturday morning from an unknown disease.

Ellis cut his light brown eyes down to slits to where their color, the color that had made him so irresistibly attractive to Fantasma all those many forgotten years ago, was barely noticeable. He grinned in a way that resembled a Laughing Jack more than it did anything close to a smile.

"Ain't gonna be a next time, Fan. You ain't gotta worry one bit about that. All you got to do is do what I say, and you get to sit your ass back down before I knock you through that wall and rattle those rotten-assed teeth outta your head. Fuck with me and see how much I'm playin'."

Far from any consideration of backing down, Fantasma flashed a grin of her own before daring to take two taunting steps forward. They both knew deep down it wasn't any remnant of love or kindness that kept them together after all these years, but rather a mutually cherished and nurtured resentment which enabled them to at least keep feeling *something*. It may not have been lovemaking, but it was the best they could do anymore.

Donatella had seen this macabre dance far too many times for one so young, to the point where she had gone blind to it all, even when it was happening right in front of her. Sometimes she would chart an escape route around her parents to her tiny bedroom at the end of the hall. There she would quietly close the door and then crawl into bed where she would scrunch herself into a tight ball underneath the sheets covered with cartoon characters. But other times she would sit there in her perch at the breakfast table and pretend to watch the spectacle, her eyes dull and lifeless as copper pennies found on the street.

Today would be different. Donatella could no longer watch her family feast on itself, and her bedroom was not far enough away from the carnage to offer the protection she really needed. In her child's mind the only way to truly escape was to *escape,* whatever that might mean for a small Black girl who would suddenly find herself all alone in a world she was convinced must hate her to allow her existence to be such a horrible thing. So while Ellis and Fantasma James began once again to circle one another faster and faster into a cyclone of violent passions and regrets, Donatella stepped down from her chair and, without saying a word, walked out the door. She walked haltingly down the hall, past the apartment doors that quickly shut and locked as she approached, and into a sun splashed street where she stood still looking up at the cloudless sky as tears began to stream down her face and she started to sob. It was the first time she had ever cried that she could remember, and it was more of a relief than anything else. The longer she cried, standing all alone on the sidewalk, the more she felt the crushing pressure that had been her lifelong passenger begin to rinse away like hardened bits of mud loosening in a stream. In the distance (although it really wasn't so far at all), she could hear the yells and screams of Fantasma and Ellis spilling into the air from an open window up above. She started to turn, but then changed her mind. Because to look back was to go back. And Donatella was not going back. Ever.

It may have been the certainty of that decision, made by an 8-year-old child no less, that opened the locks to what would become the rest of her life. After what felt like days of tears but was probably no longer than five minutes (because would all those grown people in a city like Detroit really stand around and watch a child cry for that long without doing something about it unless. . . maybe they knew who she. . . wasn't she that child who. . . ?)

Donatella gathered herself, like someone much older, then blinked twice. Hard.

"Hi."

The small, bright voice, sounding like bells ringing in a soft wind, came from her right. She appeared to be a few years older than Donatella, just shy of being a teen. Her smile was chocolate and warm, and Donatella loved the unusual way the multi-colored beads were zig-zagged into her shoulder-length braids. Her eyes were black, almost too black, which made the white pearls of her teeth seem to flash.

"Hi," she said again, this time taking a step closer and leaning forward, one eyebrow raised semi-comically.

She grinned. Donatella grinned back. The girl extended a hand. Several moments passed before Donatella took the girl's hand in her own. Nodded.

"Maura," the girl said.

"OK," said Donatella, to which Maura laughed.

"So is that your name then? Your name is *OK?*"

Feeling like maybe she was being laughed at, Donatella snatched her hand away and started to run/walk down the street in the other direction from the girl with wind chimes in her voice. She could feel the tears trying to force their way through the corners of her eyes once again, but she denied their efforts. Already she knew the weakness of tears, and there could be no weakness in her from this day forward.

"Wait!"

Donatella didn't wait, nor did she look back. However she did hear the rapid approach of footsteps gaining on her before she felt the light squeeze of fingers on her shoulder, and she slowed her escape.

"Girl, I'm *sorry*. I didn't mean. . . look, can we just start over? I didn't mean to say nothing to hurt you or nothin' like that. I just wanna be your friend. I know your name ain't OK. That ain't *nobody's* name."

Donatella slowed her pace further until she came to a complete stop near the end of the block. The girl's hand was still on her shoulder, light as a butterfly, as Donatella closed her eyes tight and lowered her head. Her small shoulders slumped.

"I don't know where I'm going," she said, her voice barely a whisper.

Maura nodded, her head tilted a bit to the side.

"Where is it you comin from? Wait. You comin from that window with all that yellin and screamin aren't you?"

Donatella nodded.

"*And I ain't goin' back,*" she said, this time her voice noticeably stronger.

Maura's hand squeezed tighter, but not as a threat.

"Nobody said anything about going back anywhere, did they? All I said was I wanna be your friend. Can we be friends?"

"Why you wanna be friends with me? You don't even know me."

Donatella heard a small giggle. The hand fell away from her shoulder.

"Turn around. Feels funny talkin' to your back like this."

Donatella opened her eyes slowly, then raised her head. Straightened her shoulders. Turned around, wearing her father's face of learned bravado.

"This is better, right?" said Maura.

Donatella smiled. She couldn't help herself.

"Never had a friend before," she said.

"Me either," said Maura. "Guess there's a first time for everything. So. . . what's your name?"

"Donatella."

Maura's eyes flashed with a gentle warmth.

"Pretty," she said.

Donatella's smile stretched a bit wider. It felt good to have a friend.

****

As the two girls stood at the corner, laughing and giggling as if they had known one another for years, two elderly men sat in wooden folding chairs by the front door of the apartment building where Donatella had recently exited with her face streaming tears. They both looked curious, and perhaps even a bit scared. The one with the cane and hair like clouds spoke first, his voice full of rust and remembrance. He nodded toward the corner.

85

"Ain't that the little girl lives with those two crazy-assed folk up there on the third floor? The ones still doin' all that hollerin?"

The other one, whose long face bore the weight of a salt and pepper beard that spilled down nearly to his lap, nodded in agreement.

"That's they daughter. Donatella. Pretty name. Mother got a pretty name too. Too bad she don't look nothin' like her name."

"Fantasma you talkin' about."

"Oh yeah. And back in her day? Brother lemme tell you. Girl filled that name *out*. Used to, but time ain't been kind to that woman. Husband either. You know Ellis, right? Little short nigger used to could fight so good for his size?"

"OK. Yeah, I remember. But look here Stone; who you figure that girl talkin' to down there at the end of the block? Donatella? Who it is you think she havin such a good time with? Cause I don't see nobody else down there 'cept her, and that chile way too young to be talkin to herself already."

Stone squinted at the sight, then reached into his shirt pocket to ease out a pack of Salem Lights. His only brand ever since those long gone days as a young man known for dressing sharp enough to draw blood. He tapped the pack against his finger, then shook one out. Reached into his right pocket, then his left before fingering the lighter. Even after all these years, Stone still needed the smoke to calm him whenever there was something out of order in his environment that made his heart start to race. After a minute, he exhaled a long, thin stream of smoke.

"Who knows what these children see, Red. Sometimes when you can't see what you wanna see in this life, you gotta paint your own picture."

As The Years Go Passing By

It wasn't until a full three days later when Donatella finally realized that nobody else could see Maura except for her. They had been spending much of their time on Belle Isle having all the fun in the world that two young girls could have. Sometimes they would run 'round and 'round the huge white marble sculpture of a fountain at the center of the park playing a form of tag where they would change direction as soon as one would tag the other. Other times they would just sit anywhere near the river, knees tucked up under their chins, and stare out at the river without saying a word. Without needing to. At night Maura would always be the one to find a safe place to sleep where they couldn't be found until the next day. There was never a need, time, or, quite frankly, any willingness to care about the strange, questioning reactions and expressions that surrounded their antics like spectators.

But on this particular third day it was a Sunday and cloudy. They were standing outside one of those small mini-marts that you only ever saw in Black neighborhoods where nobody paid attention to things like expiration dates and stuff like that. Either you wanted a thing or you didn't, so don't waste your time with questions. Donatella had felt her stomach starting to rumble (how had she not felt hungry for three whole days?), and Maura, hearing the sound, suggested they depart from the island for the day and find something to fill that emptiness.

"They have pretty good stuff in here," said Maura, as the two of them stood by the entrance appearing slightly grubby from three days without a bath, a shower, a comb or a change of clothes.

"Like what?" asked Donatella. "I'm really hungry."

"Yeah. I can tell. Sorry. I should have gotten you something before. I kinda forgot."

Donatella's face rearranged itself into a puzzle.

"How come *you* not hungry, Maura? You haven't eaten anything either, unless you snuck something one of those nights when I was 'sleep."

Maura looked mock-offended, then laughed.

"Little girl, what makes you think I would ever do anything like that to you? We sisters, you and me."

The puzzle relaxed into a cautious smile.

"For real? But it's only been three days!"

"Somebody tell you it's supposed to take longer than that?"

Donatella giggled, then shook her head.

"Naw."

"Good. I didn't think so. 'Cause there ain't no rules to this thing out here. There's just makin' it and not makin' it. And you and me? Together? We gonna *make it*. Now we gotta get you something to eat. C'mon, follow me."

"But you got money though? 'Cause I don't have any."

Maura gave her new sister a sly smile and a wink as the two of them followed an older gentleman inside.

"Money's overrated," she said.

"But. . ."

"*Shhhhhhhh*. C'mon. Time to teach you something. Hey, you want a Honey Bun? You want *two?*"

Donatella nodded her head enthusiastically.

"They're over there, down that row. You go ahead and grab you a couple, and whatever else you want, then meet me by the cash register, OK?"

Donatella cocked her small head to the side, her face once again a puzzle. Maura shook her head in exasperation, then gave her friend a mischievous shove toward the Honey Bun aisle.

"Go *on*. I got this. You worry too much."

So Donatella made her way to the aisle on the far side of the store, grabbed what she wanted, then walked stiffly toward the direction of the cash register. Her eyes were focused on the floor, her fingers squeezing her treats a bit too tight. There were two people in front of her; that same elderly man they had followed into the store, and a tall teenager with thick dreadlocks hanging to the middle of his back. But then her gaze swept by them both to the young brown-skinned girl working the register.

Actually, it wasn't the young girl who drew Donatella's attention. It was Maura, arms folded across her chest, sneaker-clad feet crossed at the ankles, looking down at the line of customers from her somewhat defiant stance as she stood *on top of the counter* next to the young girl who didn't seem to notice anything unusual.

Maura winked.

"Told you I got this," she said to her audience of one. No one else acted as if they heard or saw a thing.

"Next," said the cashier, as the elderly gentleman stepped forward and placed two bottles of soda on the counter, right beside Maura's feet, then asked for a pack of cigarettes. The cashier calmly reached behind her for a pack of Kools, asked if that would be all, then rang up the purchase and smiled.

"You have a good day, Mr. Brown."

"You too, baby," he said, then walked out the door.

When it came Donatella's turn, she felt her heart starting to race. She paused for a moment, thinking maybe she should step out of line and take her breakfast buns back to the aisle and leave the store before she got herself embarrassed or worse. What was Maura doing? Didn't she say they were like sisters now?

"I sure did," said Maura, her voice sounding. . . different. Like there was an echo to it.

And that's when Donatella noticed two things that didn't make sense: Maura had just answered something Donatella hadn't even said, and the cashier looked like she was frozen in place. She also looked scared.

"Little girl. Are you *sure* there isn't anything else you want outta here? 'Cause you can have anything you want, and don't worry about none of *them*. You can see they ain't movin', right? And they won't remember a thing about you or me once we're gone and they pick up where they left off."

"But how did you. . . ? Did you hurt them?"

Maura laughed, then took four steps off the counter right into the air, where she stood looking down at her friend with a look of amusement before slowly floating down beside her.

"Just because I'm a witch don't mean I like to hurt people. That's just the way they make it seem like in the movies. C'mon, let's go."

"Wait. You're a. . ."

"Girl, let's *go*. I'll explain all that later. All you need to know right now is that I'm your friend, and that I'm a *good* witch, OK? Anything I do is just to help folks. Sometimes I make mistakes, and OK sometimes I get mad, but I'm way better at controlling my temper than I used to be."

But as Donatella was to learn over the years, as their friendship blossomed into a true sisterhood, that wasn't exactly true. Which meant she had to work hard to convince herself that it *was* true. Because Maura had saved her life, which meant she owed her, which meant believing Maura was actually a sort of monster wasn't something she could live with.

And she didn't. Maura saw to that.

Just Two Girls All Grown Up. The Beauty and the Queen

As the two sisters made their way through the sometimes difficult years that followed, it was especially difficult for Donatella who at a very young age suddenly found herself raising herself together with the help of another very young girl who had revealed herself to be a witch and therefore was unlike any other young girl—or human being—that Donatella had ever met. Sometimes, as much as she hated to admit it, she did miss her parents, as crazy and violent as they could sometimes be. But at least when she was living with them, she felt more. . . *normal.* Not like some sort of vagabond with nowhere to call home, a situation which Maura seemed to thrive in and couldn't quite understand why living in such a way would sometimes throw Donatella into one of her moods. Usually she could see it coming, like a storm cloud on the horizon, and she would simply exit herself from the abandoned house they had taken over and claimed as their own (which Maura had managed to decorate like a dollhouse palace on

the inside) and take a long walk until she could feel inside
that the clouds were lifting from her sister's troubled soul.

But on this one particular summer day, Maura stared
in frustration at her sister, feeling as if maybe Donatella was
becoming a bit spoiled. Especially after all she had tried to
do for the girl all these years; liberating her from those
crazy parents, giving her a place to stay, always making sure
she never had to go hungry and had decent clothes to wear.
The one she sometimes called Little Girl would *never* have
made it out here in the wilds of the city without Maura's
street smarts—and her magic.

And so, as Donatella sat there in silence on the floor,
legs crossed, her delicate fingers twisting and then
untwisting her locks, Maura made the decision that today
would not be another long walk. Today things were going
to change. Today she was going to make Donatella see just
how good things could be for two outcast sisters like
themselves.

Tonight they were going to crash a party.

"Wait. . . we're gonna do *what?*" asked Donatella.

"We're gonna crash a party! It'll be fun! There's
gonna be dancing and music and. . . "

"But why do we have to *crash* the party? Can't we get
somebody to invite us so we'll know they want us there?
Don't you maybe know a way we could get somebody to
give us an invite?"

"But what fun would that be?"

It was a little before noon, and the two sisters were
sitting across from each other inside their living room in
their brand new home. The story behind the brand new
home went like this; the pair had been walking in tense
silence down the sidewalk in front of the dilapidated house
that leaned uncomfortably to the left like a drunk. They had

just finished having an argument a few blocks back about whether they should get a puppy—Donatella for, Maura against—when Maura suddenly stopped, her eyes lighting up. Donatella knew this could either be a very good thing or a very bad thing, so her voice was cautious and a bit edgy when she broke the silence.

"What?" she said.

"We're home," answered Maura.

And so just like that it was as if the argument had never happened. But there never was a puppy.

It wasn't the first time Maura had made that declaration about finding home. They had occupied any number of odd circumstances for days, weeks or months before deciding it was time to move on. But the affection that warmed her voice about the drunken house was the first time Maura had given any hint that this could be a more permanent stay. She used her magic to fully decorate the inside (the outside remained the same so as not to draw attention) with all sorts of colorful paintings that never hosted the same scene for more than an hour, glass sculptures that restlessly twisted, stretched and experimented in and out of new and different shapes and other artwork that similarly refused to behave. Just like Maura.

Where had she learned about all that?

"But what fun would that be?" Maura repeated, her voice now somewhat agitated as she began to levitate.

Maura was agitated (again) because she was growing tired of too often feeling like a babysitter when what she wanted was someone who could be as mischievous and carefree and adventurous as she considered herself to be. Caution to Maura was a bad word, but it was a word that Donatella practically lived by. She loved her adopted sister dearly; she had chosen her! But something would have to change. Maybe she should stop calling her Little Girl. . . ?

Donatella took note of how Maura was now floating, which was something she tended to do whenever she got upset. That day at the gas station store, when she saw her take several steps forward off the cashier's counter into the air, it had scared her. Not a lot, but enough. Now it was just. . . whatever. Maura being Maura.

"OK. Well then let me ask you this, sis: why do you wanna go to a party where won't nobody be able to see you? What fun would *that* be? Huh? Answer me that."

The last thing Donatella had ever wanted to do was to cause Maura any pain, not because she was necessarily afraid of what that might unleash, but because of affection. You didn't willingly cause pain for those you loved, even when they made you mad, and Maura was the only person she loved besides her parents, whom she hadn't seen in five years. But the gnarled expression on Maura's face told her she had maybe just crossed a line, and her heated gaze began to cool. She fumbled nervously with her fingers in her lap as she traced the patterns on the floor tile with her eyes.

"Sorry," she said, her voice sounding muffled as she shook her head. "That's not what I meant."

"Sure it is," said Maura. "But that's OK. We're still going. I think maybe you need this fun more than I do, and I need it *bad.*"

The uncomfortable silence between them lingered before Donatella slowly raised her head and met the sting of her sister's eyes with a look of apology. She shrugged.

"OK. Sure. What time?"

Maura eased one corner of her lip upward into a mischievous smile.

"Late."

Donatella thought by 'late,' Maura probably meant maybe nine or ten? But when nine o'clock came, and then ten o'clock ticked away while the couple was still sitting outside on their front steps, Donatella started to wonder if maybe the plans had changed. But the party was Maura's idea so she figured it didn't make sense to sound anxious or to push her too much. Because Maura wasn't one to recover quickly from a slight, even if it had been unintended. Best to try and relax and let Maura take the lead—wherever that may or may not take them.

"Nice night," she said.

Maura pulled out a cigarette from the pack lying on the worn step between them, lit it, then blew out a long, slow stream of smoke. She nodded, although she looked as if she hadn't heard. But then she said, "We should get ready."

It was a full half day after Maura had announced they were going to crash the party when the pair showed up at a new spot in the Boston Edison neighborhood called The Congregation. Once upon a time, in a whole other Detroit, the wine-red brick building had been a church catering to an entirely different type of congregation, which explained the name. It had become mad popular from the day the doors opened, both with the newer residents as well as the old. Tonight the spot was pulsing with the thump of house music as a swirl of multi-colored bodies bounced to the insistent beat. The crowd spilled out a pair of wide doors onto a large wooden patio that descended to a spacious backyard populated by wood-frame picnic tables overshadowed by patio umbrellas.

Donatella and Maura looked at each other, and their faces blossomed.

"You still think we're gonna have a problem getting in?" asked Maura.

Donatella laughed.

"This is so *cool!* But seriously, wouldn't it be more fun for you if everyone could *see* you? I mean, you're so pretty, Maura, and I just think. . ."

Maura gave a sly grin.

"Watch this."

Maura wore a loose-fitting, near-transparent blue and white blouse with wildly oversized sleeves, so when she raised her slender arms upward (dramatic and slow, so as to make an impression), they flapped loosely in the evening breeze like the wings of a bird preparing for flight.

Then she winked.

And then there was that white girl who was leaving the party, her clumsily joyful demeanor somewhat amplified by a collection of helpful substances playing tag inside her brain. She was with a friend, an Asian girl who appeared to be a bit more stable and who lightly held white girl's elbow, steering her past and through the animated crowd in the Congregation backyard toward the sidewalk. They were both giggling about a shared amusement, not paying much attention to Donatella and Maura who were headed the opposite direction *into* the party and were directly in their path.

Until Maura simply appeared. Right there under the streetlight. Right beside Donatella. Which was where she had been all along except. . . well. . .

Since Donatella could always see Maura, she didn't notice anything different at first and was about to ask her "Watch *what?*", but then she noticed the shocked expression on the white girl's face who had just witnessed Maura somehow just. . . *appear* right in front of her. The girl with Asian features hadn't noticed because at that moment she was looking over her shoulder trying to locate the origin of an angry shout she heard barking out of the crowd. White girl slowed down, shook her elbow loose from her friend, and was raising her arm to point at Maura, who slowly shook her head in warning as she placed a bejeweled finger to her lips.

Shhhhhhhh.

White girl's expression changed from one of fear to confusion and then faded to blank.

"Hey, are you OK?" her friend asked, her attention refocused after feeling her hand being shoved away from the elbow. White girl nodded, her eyes cloudy.

"I think we better get you home," she said.

"Yes, you probably should," agreed Maura, with a concerned smile. "She's had quite the night. Looks like a good party though, right?"

The Asian girl wore polished black boots, cutoff jeans and a black T-shirt that read "Evolution Before Revolution" in large all cap white letters. She returned the smile and nodded.

"Hey, you know how things get at Jan's parties sometimes, right? Did you know about the one next week? At that mansion in Palmer Woods?"

Maura shook her head.

"Hadn't heard. Gonna be a good one?"

"*Girl.* Not to be missed. This is gonna be the one."

Maura turned to look at Donatella, who was glaring at her and obviously dying to say something.

"She says it's not to be missed, Donnie! We should make plans."

"Hey, maybe we'll see you there! Well, I'd better get this one home. She isn't looking too good. Kinda strange though, you know? I mean, she was having such a good time and I couldn't shut her up even if I tried. And now *this*. Oh well. Maybe she just needs to sleep it off."

Maura nodded sympathetically.

"Yeah. Sleep always helps. See you."

"Bye."

Maura and her new friend exchanged farewell waves before the Asian girl and her friend made their way down the sidewalk and into the night.

"They must have parked a ways away," observed Maura, her voice sounding distant. "*Wow.* Look at all these cars."

"So when were you going to tell me?" blurted Donatella, not quite yelling but several notches above her normally shy voice.

Maura giggled.

"Just waiting for the right time, I guess. I thought it would be a fun surprise for tonight."

"Maura, we've been together for five years. *Five years.* All that time you've been acting like you didn't have any choice in being invisible and. . . no. Wait. Because here's what's more important: you and me? We're supposed to be sisters. It's what you always say. What you said first. And that should mean something. And now I'm finding out your biggest secret after all this time at a party?"

Maura reached out, trying to calm Donatella down.

"Being invisible is just more fun, that's all. I didn't think it was a big thing, OK? I didn't. I just thought. . ."

Donatella snatched herself away. She shook her head, eyes heated.

"I don't believe you sometimes."

"Donnie. . . wait. . ."

But she wouldn't. Instead, she whirled around and disappeared into the throbbing embrace of the crowd. Maura started to follow, looking like a sad puppy, then shrugged her shoulders as she watched her sister disappear. The two remained at an estranged distance for a long while, far enough apart not to be together but close enough to still be a visible presence. Donatella didn't seem to mind the distance at all and, in fact, seemed to bloom as the warmth and nearness of all those bodies moving to the beat gave birth to something inside, something that had never had the chance to be born until now. Turns out Maura wasn't the only one hiding a surprise, and she watched at first with sadness, and then a growing anger and resentment as she noticed how so many of the young men at the party found themselves attracted to Donatella. Asking her to dance, if she wanted something to drink, if there was *anything* they could do to gain her affection. Donatella would just smile, sometimes laugh, letting herself dance and sway with her eyes closed, which only drew them closer.

Why had she chosen this night to step into her beauty? Because there was no doubting how beautiful she truly was with her coffee-and-cream colored complexion, almond-shaped green eyes, and full curves. Maura had to wonder how she had not allowed herself to pay more attention when this change had taken place. And she simmered about the unfairness of it all. Because, after all, how could Donatella have ever survived without Maura? Wasn't Maura the one who rescued her from. . . *everything?* And to now be subjected to so much ingratitude and disrespect. Didn't Donnie know she could have *never* achieved that beauty without Maura keeping her safe? Keeping her fed and clothed?

Never.

Maura smiled. And then, in a hiss of smoke and flame, she disappeared. The chill of her laughter lingered longer.

The Reckoning

Donatella returned home in the early dawn hours, just as the darkness was creeping away. She hummed a tune to herself as she stepped into and inside a darkness without light or sound. It was a darkness that plugged her ears and blinded her eyes, stole her sense of smell. She couldn't feel the floor beneath her feet, or if there was anything beneath her feet at all, except more darkness. In the blink of an eye, she had been swallowed into a nothingness so complete that her rapidly escalating fear did not possess the ability to match the true dimensions of a horror that slowly sucked her into a state of being that her mind thought might be death, but her remaining consciousness recognized as something far worse. Reflexively, she tried to scream for what felt like hours, to the point where her parched throat ached from the fruitless effort. Then she simply went silent and limp, waiting for an ending she assumed must be on its way.

That's when she heard the voice, scratching inside her skull like a rat trying to eat its way out. Could it have been Maura? Possibly, there *was* a familiarity, something vaguely recognizable beneath the skin-crawling tones, but it was just a hint of someone—or something—she might have known. Maybe in another life. But now what she heard was the aural embodiment of hatred, and that hatred was directed at her.

But why? What had she ever done to spark such strong emotions? Until tonight, Donatella had only whispered through life, barely being noticed by anyone except Maura, and being just fine with that. Because she hadn't ever felt like she needed to be noticed by anyone else until tonight. Before this one special night, having her one true friend was all she ever needed. So if this was some perversion of her beloved Maura. . .

It's time, Little Girl.

Maura?

Something pulsed in the silence, like a muffled heartbeat. An affirmation.

Maura, please. I'm scared. What is this? Why is this? I don't. . .

Shhhhhh.

Maura. . .

You're all grown up now, Little Girl. I didn't want to see it, but I do now. I thought it was you and me forever, but that was silly. Since when has anyone ever granted a wish to a witch?

But can't we leave whatever this is and. . .

This is ME, Little Girl. This darkness is ME. I thought you should know who your Maura really is before I'm gone. You didn't like it when I let people see the costume of my flesh, when I tried to become more like you, so maybe it's better you remember me as I am. As all witches are. We are the sisters of darkness between the light. I saw something in you, Donatella. I thought the time would come when you could join me completely. Could join us. I loved you, Donnie. But love is the one thing that can kill a witch quicker than any other. I always knew that, but I wasn't willing to accept it.

But you're my only friend. What am I supposed to do without. . . how am I supposed to survive? Where am I supposed to go?

Slowly, the suffocating darkness began to fade and break apart like clouds abandoning a storm, revealing the scattered details of the home Donatella had thought she was returning to. The home Maura had made for them both. Only now it was just Donatella, warm tears streaming down her face as she crumpled to the floor and began to sob.

"Where am I supposed to go?"

The Truth and Marcellus

Her voice was no longer raping the insides of my skull, but having this thing toy with me using Mom's voice was far worse. I resisted the urge to lunge at the swirling mass of flesh and fluid because I figured that's what she wanted. Also, because I could hear the memory of my real mother's voice warning me against making a decision that could get me killed—or worse. I had never considered the possibility that there could be much of anything worse than death, but as I experienced this surreal scenario taking place during what was supposed to be my lunch break, it occurred to me that death might be far preferable to whatever kind of eternal pain this thing might have the power to inflict.

"Yeah. Just look at me," I said sarcastically. "Who could ask for anything more than where I am right now?

"You could, Marcellus. That's who. You could ask for anything you want, dear heart."

I was standing there inside that huge, breathing bubble she had wrapped around us both, where I could watch the lunchtime crowd walking back and forth on the other side. It was like looking through a funhouse mirror as their shapes morphed in and out of various configurations, and none of them even noticed either me or this. . . *thing. . .* that was only a few feet away.

And that's when I knew.

"It was you who killed my mother, wasn't it?"

For the first time during our encounter, for the briefest moment, the witch looked uncertain, as if she expected something to happen. Maybe she expected me to lunge at her. But even if I had the power to kill her, which I knew I didn't, it wasn't her death that would give me what I needed at that moment.

"You said I could ask for anything I want, right?"

The witch just stared, I could tell already regretting her offer.

"So I'm guessing you already know forgiveness is off the table. What I *do* want is an answer; why did you wait so long? Why did you wait until she had a life? Until she had *me?* Why did you have to wait until you could hurt us both? Did you really hate my mother so much?"

The witch shook her head.

"If I had hated your mother, then I never would have left, Dear Heart. I left because I loved her, and that's also why I came back. I came back because the love I had for your mother wouldn't die. And so I thought. . ."

"But why did you kill her?"

Slowly, painfully, that wretched thing that had first presented itself to me as a homeless woman stretched, pulled, and contorted bone and muscle until a slightly built woman with skin the color of dark chocolate was standing there looking at me with this expression that couldn't seem to make up its mind whether it was hostility or fear. She wore a loose-fitting autumn-colored gown with wide sleeves that draped to the ground, and she had this short silvery afro that seemed to float on top of her scalp, the way seaweeds wave underwater.

"Your mother loved me," she said.

"Maybe so. But then that makes me want to know even more why you would want to kill her."

I could tell she was weighing whether or not to answer me, or maybe she was deciding whether to tell me the truth. And then. . .

"I killed your mother because I couldn't forget her."

That's when I smiled, which confused the witch.

"You know what my mother always told me?"

She shook her head.

"No."

"My mother always told me that the dead stay with you longer than the living. And now I know what it is I want. That is, if you're a witch of your word."

"And what is that?" she asked, trying to hide the nervousness in her voice.

"Kill me."

A DSQ Special Feature

Last edition we presented a story created entirely from the Artificial Intelligence program ChatGPT. So popular was it that we've decided to make it a regular feature. Before we get to that, however, please note our standing policy about AI use:

ANY story that has either been generated by AI or where the author has used AI in any way shape or form as part of the creative process will be noted (e.g., see AI Disclosure at the conclusion of "Midnight Mercy"). We still believe that as amazing as AI may be, the creativity of human beings and the human imagination should *never* be replaced by artificial human creations.

Okay…now, enjoy "The Portal at Detroit"!

The Portal at Detroit
By ChatGPT

The following is an AI-generated story. Though the prompt was refined, here is the general wording: "Please create a historical science fiction story set in Detroit, ca. 1859, about an immortal who has lived on earth for thousands of years and an Alien businessman from the Alpha Centauri galaxy. Include a young boy who will have his own story. There is a meeting to establish a time portal."

The Restaurant Beyond Time

The bell above the door jingled in the ordinary street of Detroit, yet inside, nothing was ordinary. Elijah Harper wiped the counter with a rag worn soft by decades of service, though he hadn't needed to do so for centuries. *Centuries.* The number felt trivial now, almost irrelevant, for Elijah had witnessed the rise and fall of empires, the shifting of continents, and the subtle, almost invisible progress of human understanding. No mortal could grasp the fullness of a lifespan like his. He had walked the earth for more than ten thousand years.

Tonight, his small restaurant, a tidy brick building tucked between a blacksmith and a tailor on Jefferson Avenue, was no ordinary restaurant. Outside, the horse-drawn wagons rattled and clattered on cobblestone streets, and lamplighters trundled down the avenues, sparking flames into oil lamps that sputtered and hissed. Inside, Elijah sat alone at a corner table, awaiting a meeting that would bend the very fabric of time and space.

The air shimmered faintly in the corner of the room, almost like heat on asphalt, yet it had no warmth. There, a bubble—transparent and impossibly dense—held two beings who should not, by any natural law, coexist in that place: a human from a century ahead, and a visitor from the Alpha Centauri galaxy. The bubble was anchored to Elijah's mind, his immemorial essence, and to no other part of the universe. Through it, he could see and hear all, yet passersby would never notice. The world outside carried on, blissfully ignorant.

Inside the bubble, the human stepped forward first. He was tall, lean, and carried the air of someone who had walked through centuries of innovation with confidence yet caution. His eyes, sharp and calculating, flicked across Elijah before resting on the being beside him: tall, iridescent, its skin shimmering in hues that humans could not name, and eyes like liquid silver, reflecting worlds beyond their comprehension.

"You said this was the right place," the human said, voice low and careful. "Detroit . . . in 1859?"

The alien nodded, each movement deliberate, graceful. "Here and now, temporal coordinates fixed. The nexus point is ready. But the question remains: is this species ready to wield what you propose?"

The human sighed, running a hand through his hair. "That is precisely my concern. Earth . . . this era . . . humanity is still mired in ignorance. The spiritual,

ethical growth required to protect such technology—"
He paused, eyes narrowing, "—it is simply not
present."

Elijah leaned back, observing them both. He had
seen the hesitancy in centuries of time travelers before,
though never one so earnest in moral judgment. He
broke the silence with a voice smooth and deep, yet
tinged with amusement:

"You speak as if humanity is a single heart
beating in unison," he said. "It is not. There are
shadows, yes . . . but there are sparks too. And
sometimes, it is the smallest spark that ignites the
whole flame."

The time traveler's eyes flickered toward him.
"You . . . you have watched, and yet you permit this
discussion?"

Elijah shrugged, a motion that carried the weight
of millennia. "I have seen empires rise and fall, kings
crowned and deposed, wars that swallowed continents .
. . and children who offered more light than any
monarch ever could. If you want to know whether
Earth is ready, perhaps we need to look closer to the
fire, not just the smoke."

The alien, shimmering, extended a limb,
translucent and impossibly elegant, toward Elijah. "He
is correct," it said. "The potential exists. You, time
traveler, fear a world of cruelty, yet even here—amid
the struggle—there are those who embody what you
claim is absent. We must seek them. Detroit, 1859, is
more than a city. It is a crucible."

Sparks Among the Shadows

Elijah guided the other two outside the bubble, though, in truth, they were already outside in plain sight. The city bustled, unaware, its streets alive with horses, wagons, and laborers calling across markets. Smoke rose from factories, blending with autumn mists. Elijah's keen eyes scanned the street, searching for the spark the alien had spoken of.

"It is not always obvious," Elijah murmured. "The flame hides in plain sight. Often, it is found in the hands of those who do not even know their own power."

The alien's head tilted, silvery eyes gleaming. "Show me."

Elijah led them down a narrow lane behind the market. There, playing with a simple wooden hoop, was a boy no more than eight years old. He laughed as the hoop rolled across the dirt path, chasing it with bare feet and a heart untroubled by the weight of injustice or history. Yet it was not just play that drew Elijah's attention—it was the way the boy stopped suddenly, noticing a stray dog tangled in a vendor's rope.

Without hesitation, the boy ran to the dog, untangling the ropes with careful fingers, whispering to calm the frightened animal. He then gave it some bread from his small lunch and guided it gently to safety.

"Observe," Elijah said quietly. "Compassion, awareness, responsibility . . . small, yes, but uncorrupted. This child carries a light the universe can recognize."

The alien's voice was soft, melodic. "This is what I hoped to find. Here is a seed that has not been poisoned by greed or fear. Here is the essence that can flourish into guardianship of a portal, if given the chance."

The human time traveler frowned. "A child . . . this is your argument? That a single human being can justify placing Earth at the center of interdimensional travel? How naive."

Elijah's eyes glimmered. "Naive? Perhaps. Or perhaps it is wise to remember that the smallest of us often shape the greatest outcomes. The world is not ready, yes . . . but some among it are ready."

The boy, oblivious to the monumental decision being weighed above him, patted the dog's head gently and sent it running back to the streets. He looked at a stray kitten perched on a cart, and without hesitation, carried it to safety as well. It was simple, mundane, and yet,

Elijah could feel the reverberation of choice and kindness, a pulse that transcended centuries.

The time traveler's face softened, the stern lines of his jaw relaxing. "Perhaps . . . perhaps the argument is not purely about society at large. Perhaps it is about what sparks exist, what guardians can be nurtured."

The alien inclined its head, and for a brief moment, its form shimmered like liquid light, reverberating with the boy's actions. "Exactly. And that is why Detroit, 1859, is not too early. The portal must have caretakers capable of perceiving the highest good, even in small hands."

The Bubble of Agreement

Back inside the restaurant, the bubble shimmered once more as the alien and the time traveler resumed their discussion. Elijah leaned against the counter, watching, listening, and occasionally offering a word to steady the more anxious human.

"You underestimate the capacity of those who do not yet rule kingdoms or own lands," Elijah said. "Children, artisans, and even those overlooked by history—they see and act differently. Their morality is not constrained by empire or profit. You may be surprised at what they can protect."

The time traveler rubbed his temples, the weight of potential responsibility pressing against him. "I am not asking for perfect humans. I am asking for . . . humans ready to bear the burden of a technology that can alter existence itself."

"Burden, yes," Elijah said. "But the same technology, handled by those with hearts capable of empathy and insight, becomes gift rather than curse. That boy . . . he is the proof."

The alien extended a silvery limb between them, almost as if bridging time and space itself. "We will seed the portal. Detroit will be its nexus. The guardianship will begin with those we identify as worthy. We are not naive. But we are not blind either. This child, this community, these sparks—these will shape the future of interdimensional travel, if given care and respect."

The time traveler exhaled, eyes narrowing as he considered the delicate balance. "If I agree . . . it is under the condition that humanity is observed and guided. They must grow spiritually as they grow technologically. Failure is unacceptable."

Elijah smiled, the corners of his eyes crinkling. "And so it shall be. I have watched humanity for more than ten thousand years. I have seen failure, yes . . . but I have also seen resilience and wonder that defy all expectation. Detroit is ready, not because of all humanity—but because of those who are ready to light the way."

The alien's voice pulsed, harmonic and warm. "Then it is done. The first stage of the interdimensional agreement will commence. The portal will be seeded, the guardians identified, and the pathways secured. Time, traveler, you will witness the beginning, not the end."

And in that moment, in the unremarkable restaurant on Jefferson Avenue, history and eternity intersected. Outside, the city carried on, unaware of the monumental covenant forged within a bubble beyond time. Inside, Elijah Harper smiled, wiping his hands on his apron, ready to serve the next customer, whether mortal, visitor, or traveler from some impossible future.

Because sometimes, the greatest acts of history are not recognized by those who live them—they are seen only by those who have already seen a thousand lifetimes, and by those who carry the light forward.

Shadows of Doubt

The bubble shimmered like liquid glass as the human time traveler paced in a circle. His boots made no sound on the restaurant floor, though Elijah could see the tension radiating off him.

"I can't help but think," the time traveler said, rubbing his forehead, "that we are rushing. The humans of 1859 are . . . chaotic. Slavery persists, greed is rampant, cities polluted, and the spiritual growth of the masses . . . stunted. How can we trust them with a portal that allows instantaneous travel across time and space?"

Elijah leaned against the counter, arms crossed, eyes calm but piercing. "You speak as though humans are a single organism, a single heartbeat," he said, his voice smooth and deliberate. "They are not. Even in the darkest hours, there are flickers—moments of courage, empathy, and moral clarity. That boy you observed—he is one of those sparks. One spark, if tended, can light an entire forest."

The alien, their form now oscillating gently like a living prism, extended a hand toward the human. "Your concern is valid. Earth is imperfect, yet imperfection does not preclude readiness. Guardians, not the entire species, will be responsible. Detroit, 1859, is the ideal crucible precisely because imperfection surrounds it. Only through contrast can the virtue of the chosen emerge."

The time traveler exhaled sharply. "And if they fail? The misuse of this technology . . . the consequences are unfathomable. Temporal disruption, interdimensional conflict, cosmic contamination—"

Elijah's eyes softened. "I have lived ten thousand years. I have seen failure, yes . . . but also the miraculous resilience of life. The boy we observed—he shows empathy beyond his years. You worry about the species at large, but I ask you to consider those who can guide it. Are we not here to identify and nurture them?"

The human paused, weighing Elijah's words. The alien shimmered, almost imperceptibly nodding, their form resonating with the truth of what Elijah had said.

The Boy's Light

Elijah led the visitors out into the street again. The boy, whose name was Samuel, was now sweeping the steps of a nearby bakery, his small hands pushing dirt and debris from the worn boards. Elijah motioned for the visitors to watch.

A stray horse-drawn cart veered slightly off course, a frightened horse kicking at the cobblestones. Samuel froze for a heartbeat, then ran forward, catching the reins before they could snap from the driver's grasp. Calmly, he soothed the horse with gentle words, steadying both beast and cart. The driver, astonished, leaned from the carriage window. "Well, young man, you saved us both!" he exclaimed.

Samuel only nodded, shyly, returning to his broom.

The alien's voice resonated, a melody that seemed to vibrate through the air itself. "Observe the pattern. Compassion, vigilance, courage. Each act small, but cumulative. These qualities form the foundation of stewardship."

Elijah smiled. "Yes. One child's choices ripple through time. This boy is unremarkable in appearance, yet extraordinary in consequence. It is the smallest sparks that sometimes ignite the largest fires."

The time traveler's gaze softened, though a shadow of doubt lingered. "And yet . . . he is a child. How can we rely on one child to represent readiness for a planet?"

Elijah's eyes twinkled. "You misunderstand. We do not rely solely on him. He is the seed. Others like him exist, scattered like stars across the centuries. Our task is to cultivate and protect these lights. And I assure you— the universe notices them."

Negotiation of the Portal

Inside the restaurant, Elijah guided the two visitors back to the table. The bubble shimmered faintly, a protective layer separating them from the ordinary world.

"Let us speak plainly," Elijah said. "The portal's placement on Earth carries enormous responsibility. But placing it where the light exists—where it can be protected and nurtured—is essential. Detroit is not chosen by geography alone; it is chosen by humanity's potential."

The alien extended a limb, and its fingers glimmered as they moved. "Our calculations show minimal risk if guardians are carefully selected. Observers will monitor, but we cannot interfere directly without breaching cosmic protocols. Earth must demonstrate capability."

The time traveler's face was grim. "Capability . . . yes. But Earth is fractured, violent, and unprepared. I have seen civilizations collapse in other timelines when trust was placed in immature societies. I cannot . . . I cannot sanction the use of a portal here lightly."

Elijah spoke slowly, choosing each word like a sculptor shaping stone. "You ask for certainty where none exists. You ask for perfection in an imperfect world. But look to what is good, what is resilient, what can be guided. Samuel—the boy—represents that spark. Others will follow, if we allow it."

The alien nodded. "His example validates the principle. Guardianship will be a mentorship system, not a reliance on naivety. Earth is ready, not fully, but in potential, and that is sufficient."

The time traveler's eyes closed for a moment, the weight of millennia pressing down on him. When he spoke again, his tone had softened. "Very well. I will sanction the initial stage, contingent on careful monitoring and guidance. Detroit, 1859 . . . shall become the first node."

The Covenant Sealed

The bubble began to expand, shimmering with radiant hues that no human could name. Elijah watched silently as the alien extended a glowing limb, tracing a circuit through the air. Symbols formed—alien, temporal, and yet intuitively comprehensible in the mind.

"This is the covenant," the alien said. "The agreement is formed. Guardians will be identified, mentorship established. Temporal and interdimensional travelers may use the nexus once protocols are in place. Earth's potential is sufficient to begin."

The time traveler exhaled and finally relaxed, a rare smile breaking the tension. "It begins, then. But the Earthlings themselves must rise to meet the challenge, guided yet free."

Elijah leaned back, hands folded. "They will. And the boy, Samuel, is only the beginning. The ripple will spread outward. Watch, traveler, and learn: the smallest acts often shape the greatest futures."

The alien shimmered, almost imperceptibly nodding. "Indeed. Detroit, 1859 . . . a seed planted in space and time. Watch carefully. Nurture, protect, and allow the light to grow."

Outside, the city continued, unaware of the covenant forged within a single restaurant. Wagons clattered, voices carried through the streets, smoke rose from chimneys, and a child laughed, chasing a wooden hoop. Yet in that laughter, Elijah could hear the universe itself resonating with possibility.

Reflections of an Immortal

Elijah returned to his apron and the counter, wiping it once more. Centuries had taught him that history is rarely shaped by the extraordinary alone—it is shaped by the ordinary, the unseen, and the patient. A child's hand saving a dog, a stranger's kindness in passing, a student's curiosity in class—these were the sparks that could ignite galaxies.

The time traveler and the alien prepared to depart, their forms folding into temporal and dimensional pathways beyond mortal comprehension.

"Remember," Elijah said quietly, "the light exists. You only need to find it, nurture it, and allow it to grow."

The human nodded, a trace of humility in his eyes. "I understand now. The universe is not just about what we see; it is about what we cultivate."

The alien's final words echoed, harmonious and eternal: "Guardianship begins in the smallest hearts. Detroit, 1859 . . . shall be remembered."

And with that, they were gone. The bubble vanished. The restaurant returned to its ordinary state. Elijah Harper stood behind the counter, a witness to history and eternity alike. Outside, the world went on, blissfully unaware.

Yet Elijah smiled. He had seen a boy, a spark, a possibility that could change everything. And in that spark, the future of Earth—and the cosmos—was secure.

Our Authors

Keith A. Owens has lived in Detroit since 1993. He has worked at a variety of newspapers across the country including The Detroit Free Press, The Michigan Chronicle, The Metro Times, and the Denver Post. Mr. Owens oversees marketing and PR for Detroit Stories Quarterly and is a co-founder. He has been a professional musician for more than two decades and has performed at the Detroit Jazz Festival, The Windsor Blues Festival, and the International Blues Competition in Memphis, Tennessee.

R.E. McTyre, Sr. is a co-founder of Detroit Stories Quarterly and is the managing editor. A Detroit-based writer, editor, and publisher, he also teaches writing, business, and technology.

Marsalis Higgs spent his childhood composing illustrated epics and giving lectures. After graduating from the University of Michigan, he published works in every literary style and genre. He is the founder of the pop music blog, Paraphernalia. He loves bubblegum, fast cars, and silent cinema

Abel Ramirez has been writing and drawing since his father, Abel Ramirez Sr., put a pencil in his hand at the age of five. His interests include writing, art, physical fitness, and martial arts. He is the founder of ALPHA-7 Athletics Wear and author of *The Ravensgate Chronicles*.

ChaptGPT is an AI language model developed by OpenAI that generates human-like text for conversation, writing, and problem-solving.

Our Stories

Our Voice

Our Way